Everybody Called
Her a Saint

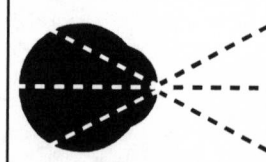

EVERYBODY'S SUSPECT IN GEORGIA,
BOOK THREE

EVERYBODY CALLED HER A SAINT

A ROMANCE MYSTERY

CECIL MURPHEY

THORNDIKE PRESS
A part of Gale, Cengage Learning

GALE
CENGAGE Learning

Detroit • New York • San Francisco • New Haven, Conn • Waterville, Maine • London

GALE
CENGAGE Learning™

LIBRARY OF CONGRESS CATALOGING-IN-PUBLICATION DATA

Murphey, Cecil.
    Everybody called her a saint : a romance mystery / by Cecil Murphey. — Large print ed.
        p. cm. — (Thorndike Press large print Christian mystery) (Everybody's suspect in Georgia; bk. 3)
    ISBN-13: 978-1-4104-2222-4 (alk. paper)
    ISBN-10: 1-4104-2222-4 (alk. paper)
    1. Georgia—Fiction. 2. Large type books. I. Title.
PS3613.U723E83 2010
813'.6—dc22
                                          2009048494

Published in 2010 by arrangement with Barbour Publishing, Inc.

For the real Twila Belk, whom I would kill only in fiction, but especially for Shirley, who is God's special gift to me.

1

If it hadn't been for Twila Belk, I wouldn't have taken the Antarctic cruise, and I wouldn't have seen Burton again. If I hadn't gone on the cruise, I wouldn't have been there when someone murdered Twila.

Twila was a special friend — unquestionably my closest friend. Even now, tears fill my eyes whenever I think about her death. "It can't be," I tell myself. "It just can't be." If she had died of natural causes, I would have mourned, but grief and shock mingled together still overpower me at times.

"Why would anyone murder Twila Belk?" I asked shortly after we learned of her death. So did the others on the cruise.

In the year or so I had known Twila, not once had I ever heard anyone say a negative word about her. If anything, almost everybody called her a saint. And she was exactly that. Even now that it's all over, she is as revered in death as she was in life.

Burton and I had broken up. That's the reason I almost didn't go on the cruise — oh yes, Burton. You won't understand all the things that happened unless I start with him. His name is James Burton the Third, but he likes everyone to call him just Burton. He's the pastor of a church in Riverdale, a small town about twenty miles south of Atlanta and about a ten-minute drive from the Hartsfield-Jackson Airport.

Our relationship was growing, and we began to talk about marriage. Almost a year earlier I had become a believer — largely through the influence of Burton, but God had also sent a few other surprises into my life. They were individuals who talked about God, as do a lot of people. But these folks lived the life they talked about. I had seen few others do that.

I'll say it straight. I loved Burton, even before I became a Christian. I had been married before, but my drug-user husband died in an accident. Burton knew about my past. I think I began to fall in love with him the evening we met on the Georgia coast when we solved the murder of Roger Harden. Sorry, I'm getting ahead of myself again. I'll try to make this a linear story.

I'm an inch taller and three years older than he is. He's never been married — lucky me. I have red hair that I call titian, and he has gorgeous black, curly hair; deep, deep blue eyes; and the kind of smile that melts me whenever I look at him.

Six weeks before the murder of Twila, I was sure we would get married. I wasn't sure I wanted to take on the role of a pastor's wife, but, hey, I could fake that part. I'm a professional — the head of Clayton County Special Services, so I worked past that part. Everything seemed so wonderful for about six weeks.

That's when I found out about his problem.

It was *his* problem — or at least he was the cause of the problem.

Weeks earlier we had one of those beautiful candlelight dinners. In one of those special places — you know, the kind of place where you don't read the right side of the menu or care about prices. I sat as demurely as it's possible for me to sit. He ordered the same meal for both of us: chicken in aspic and asparagus. The presentation on the plate was probably as good as the meal itself.

I knew he would propose, and I thought of at least twelve ways to sound extremely surprised. In the end, I thought a simple yes would be enough.

But I never said yes.

I knew he had bought a ring for me. I learned that from his secretary, who thought I already knew.

He didn't have some kind of wacky presentation by the server, such as sticking the ring inside my coeur de crème over wild strawberries. I hadn't expected anything like that from Burton.

After dinner we drove toward my apartment. He switched on the CD player and we listened to those old, old Tony Bennett songs like "Because of You" and "A Stranger in Paradise." He had done that for atmosphere, and I didn't want to spoil anything. He parked in front of my building, shut off the engine, but kept the music going. It was on the second playing of "Because of You." We listened in silence until that song finished.

"I have something to tell you," he said.

I held back from saying, "At last." To enhance the softness of the moment, I said nothing but clasped his hand.

"I love you, Julie. I don't know if it's your smart mouth or your quick thinking, but I love you. I love everything about you."

I kissed his cheek. I wasn't going to say yes until he asked. But I had practiced the word a thousand times.

"I want to marry you —"

Something wasn't right about the way he said that. Was there a *but* at the end of that sentence?

"I — I have a secret. It's something I've never told anyone else —"

"Funny. That's what all my clients say."

"But this is different."

"Would you believe I hear that statement about once a week in my practice?"

"This is — this is something — something important —"

I had three or four smart-mouthed answers fighting to pop out of my mouth, but once again, I shut up.

For a long time, Burton said nothing. I reached over and turned off the CD. It didn't seem right to hear that soft, romantic music right now.

I don't think it was my flip remarks; I think he was quiet because it was so difficult for him to speak about his dark past. I couldn't see his features clearly in the semidarkness, and after a few more seconds of silence, I wondered if I had said the wrong thing. He said he loved my smart mouth, didn't he? Yet I knew it was better to keep quiet and let him work through whatever conflict he had.

After two or three more minutes of silence,

he said, "You remember when we met at Palm Island?"

"Do you think I have amnesia?" was what I wanted to say. Instead, I nodded. "Every person there had a secret —"

"Which was the reason we were there."

"Roger Harden knew all the secrets, and —"

Burton held up a hand. "Everybody's secret came out."

"I remember."

"Everybody's secret except mine."

"That's right!" I had forgotten. From across the room in Roger's house, I had formed the question, "You, too?" with my lips and he'd nodded. "You never told me what it was."

"I was too ashamed."

"All of us on that island were ashamed. That's why we all had secrets." I realized that he hadn't been as self-revealing as I had assumed. That hurt, and I'm sure he caught the sadness in my voice.

"I want to tell you now."

He melted me again. And I did love him, so I took his hand and whispered, "I love you. I doubt that anything —"

"You haven't heard yet."

I decided to listen to him bare his soul. I loved him and was sure nothing would

12

change my attitude toward him.

"I did tell one person — Roger Harden. But you must have assumed that. Roger's dead, so no one else in the world knows."

I rubbed his cheek softly. I didn't want to spoil the intimacy of the moment with any words, no matter how tender they sounded.

That night Burton told me his long-held secret. His words horrified me. I couldn't believe I loved a man who would commit such a harsh, cruel, and selfish act. He admitted that it had been sinful and self-centered, and he had never been able to tell the truth about it.

"You have to make this right," I said. "You're a Christian and a preacher. You're supposed to tell me to do things like that."

"I can't. Don't you see I can't do this to *them?*"

"I hate what you did!" My words surprised me. Part of it was the shock, but more than that, the confession came from a man I loved — the man I planned to marry. Okay, the confession came from a man I thought was only two short steps away from perfection.

"Besides — besides, it's too late!"

"It is never too late to right a wrong. I've even heard you say that. I can't believe —" I broke off, and tears filled my eyes. How could he have done such a horrible thing? Worse, how could he have lived with himself since then?

"You don't understand," he said, but without much force in his words. I think he knew he had lost not only my respect but my love.

"You're right, I don't understand. I don't want to understand." I reached for the door handle. "Don't call me again," I said.

"Please —"

"Maybe you can salve your conscience by confessing to me, but that's — that's not good enough! I can't marry you. I feel —" I was so angry and so horrified I couldn't finish my sentence. I slammed the door and ran to my apartment. I was such an emotional mess that it took me four tries before I could get my key into the lock.

I didn't stop loving him, but I tried. I decided that the only way to get past my feelings was to get away from him.

That was the last time I saw Burton until the cruise.

2

Less than a week after I broke up with Burton, I moved out of my apartment in Riverdale and rented one in Jonesboro. It was only ten minutes away from him but far enough so I wouldn't run into him at a supermarket or gas station. I didn't go back to that church — I couldn't sit in a pew and listen to him speak. I visited several other churches a few times, but I wasn't ready to join any of them. Besides, when Burton preached, his words had a way of making me examine my heart. No other minister had been able to make me feel that way.

I felt I needed to focus on one thing — getting on with my life — and that meant getting Burton out of it. But such goals aren't always that easy to reach. It certainly wasn't for me.

In time I might have been able to get away from Burton if it hadn't been for Twila Belk and the Antarctic cruise. For nearly three months, she had focused her energies on that once-in-a-lifetime trip. She had spent an immense amount of money for a fourteen-day excursion. It wasn't typical of her to be obsessed with something like that, but whenever she phoned me (at least once every day), the cruise was the top subject of conversation, and when she e-mailed me (almost every day), she expressed new anxieties about the trip.

Although the cruise seemed unlike the things she normally did, I loved her enough that I decided to put up with her strange behavior. She had reserved all forty-eight places on a ship named the *Vaschenko,* which had once been some kind of Russian deep-sea research vessel. After the end of the cold war, it had been refitted as a tourist ship. Most of the cabins contained two bunk beds; a few handled four. She took one cabin to be totally alone — which I didn't understand at the time. But it was her money to do with as she chose.

I didn't know every person on the list, but she assured me that wasn't going to be a problem. We'd be together for fourteen days aboard a small ship. I'd get to know them all before we returned.

Two weeks before the cruise, I drove by

Twila's office to tell her that I had decided not to go. She was already aware that I had broken up with Burton, and I assumed she would understand. I hadn't given her any details except the usual catch-up phrases about incompatible temperaments. I called her and said I wanted to talk to her, and it was important. She said her last client would be gone by five, so I arrived five minutes after that.

She probably anticipated why I had come to see her. At least she didn't seem surprised when I said, "Twila, I love you, but I can't go on the cruise. I've thought about this quite a bit. It would be too painful for me to be on the same cruise with Burton."

"Don't waste any words working up to the topic, my dear." She laughed with that wonderfully deep, hearty laugh. "That's one quality I like about you, Julie. You say it straight."

"So now you know why I can't go on the trip."

"Oh no," she said. "I refuse to let you back out."

"You refuse?" Then I laughed. "That's one quality I dislike about you. You won't let the topic drop."

"All but a few of you on the cruise are special. I feel close to you and want to be

17

with you," she said. "Some are former or present clients. About a dozen are close friends. You're number one on the list."

Her directness disconcerted me. To stall until I could figure out a good retort, I asked, "What about the others?"

"You know how it is when you have a party, don't you? You end up inviting a few people out of obligation, or because they beg for an invitation."

"So you'll have some of them on the cruise?"

"A few," Twila said and sighed. "I'm thankful there are only a few."

Twila was a short, older woman and still trim. I don't think she had ever been beautiful, but her even features made her attractive. Time had been kind to her, and she had let it do its own work. Twila's once-blond hair had turned a silvery gray. The lines on her face weren't the etched strokes of sadness; rather, they formed patterns of contentment as if she were always happy. Her honey-brown eyes made me feel that a woman of twenty hid inside a body of someone forty years older. That day she wore a cream silk blouse, black silk slacks, and low-heeled shoes. She tied her hair back with a ribbon of black moiré silk.

Excitedly she told me (probably for the

fiftieth time during the past month) that she had planned the cruise around the people who were truly special in her life. "So except for those obligatory individuals, my guests are people I love or individuals who have been of deep spiritual influence in my life."

"And that list of special people includes Burton?"

"You were first on my list. Burton was second."

"I'm sorry, but you'll have to delete my name." I said those words to her in the strongest, no-nonsense voice I could muster. "I'm sure you'll have no problem getting someone to fill my half cabin."

"It's not a matter of getting someone to sleep in your bunk," she said. "I want *you*."

"I can't."

"Yes, you can. I refuse to accept your declining the invitation," she said. I can't explain the timbre of her voice, but once in a while — and quite rarely — Twila said something with a gravity in her voice that Moses probably would have loved to emulate on Mount Sinai. "You will go."

"I can't. Please don't ask me again. I love you, but I can't." My pain over Burton was stronger than obeying an all-but-divine command. In a rush of painful words, I reminded her that Burton and I had broken up. I said I couldn't divulge the reason because that was for him to tell her. Twila, my friend, was also a professional, and I knew she would never probe once I set the boundary.

After I finished the torrent of words, Twila stared at me for several seconds. She shifted her gaze into space, and I sensed she was trying to decide what to say to me.

"I'm not going. It's that simple," I said.

"I've never asked anything of you in the months we've known each other." Before I could come up with a flippant response, she said, "This is one thing I ask of you. Please. You have become — I suppose I'd have to say like my own daughter. I've planned every detail of this trip, and it's extremely important."

"Important?" I asked. "What makes it important? Antarctica would be wonderful, but I would hardly call it important."

"It is important. *To me.*"

"This is so untypical of you."

"That's correct," she said. Her lips trembled ever so slightly before she said, "Julie, my dear one, this is the last, most important thing I shall do in my life."

That may sound like the tone of a martyr as I tell it, but it came across as a declaration — much like someone who says, "This is the last project I'll take on before I quit this job."

Although I heard the intensity, I wasn't ready to capitulate. "But don't you see? Burton will be on the ship, as well. I — I can't face him. I don't want to be around him —"

"There will be nearly fifty passengers on the *Vaschenko.* You'll see him, but you will not have to talk to him on any personal level or be anywhere near him."

"I can't. I love you, Twila, but I — I can't. Please understand."

Twila turned her head away — and that gesture hurt more than anything she said. "I beg you. Please."

I had never heard her talk like that. She was one of those cheerful, upbeat types, and nothing ever seemed to upset her. I decided to choose my words carefully. Maybe if she knew his secret, she'd understand. "You see, Twila —"

As if she hadn't heard me, she said, "I want you to know why this is so important to me and why I want you — why I need you — on the ship with me: I don't expect to live more than a few more months."

3

I didn't know what to say when Twila told me she would die within the year. I must have looked as if I were frozen, but I couldn't take in her words.

She grabbed my hand. "I've decided to tell you — only you — and you must not tell anyone. Promise me that?"

Still unable to speak because of the shock, I nodded.

"I have cancer. You remember shortly after we met, I told you that three years ago I underwent a mastectomy."

Again a mute response from me.

"It's back, and it has metastasized." She went into a medical explanation — she was an MD who specialized in psychiatry. Except for her personal physician, an oncologist, no one else knew how aggressively the cancer had spread. "Nothing has worked. We doctors do what we can, but sometimes God overrules."

"No, no —"

"These things are in the hands of God," she said. "I am at peace."

"You can't — you can't die —"

"Please, my dear. If you must argue, argue with God. I've made my peace with Him." She smiled and said, "I'll soon be with my Otto and Reinhard."

I knew who she meant. She and Otto Belke (which he shortened to Belk because people couldn't pronounce the short *e* in German) married shortly after both of them had finished their residencies at Johns Hopkins in Baltimore. Otto bought a partnership with two other surgeons in Clayton County. Twila went into private practice.

Twelve years later, Otto and their only child, Reinhard, died when a truck's brakes failed at seventy miles an hour and rammed their car into a concrete abutment. Twila had been hospitalized for weeks with a broken pelvis. Her right leg never healed quite right, and she walked with a barely noticeable limp.

"Shh, no tears," Twila said. "Please don't shed tears for me. I am going to that perfect place we sing about in church."

The truthfulness of her voice made the tears slide more rapidly down my cheeks.

Twila is going to die soon.

No, it can't be.

"You're only sixty-one. You're so spry and filled with life —"

"You wish to argue with God, is that it?" Twila smiled, and it wasn't a false smile. The deep inner peace was obvious.

"I can't accept that. There are other treatments and —" She stopped me before I could suggest she get a second opinion.

"This is my body. I know it is breaking down, and I'm ready." She took my hand again and held it. "We shall never speak of this again."

"But I can't —"

"I've told you because the trip to Antarctica is to fulfill my last dream. When we first married, Otto and I decided that one day we would go to Antarctica together. I must go. This is the last chance. Otto can't go with me, but I can take the friends who are the dearest to my heart." She seemed unaware that her nails dug into my hand, but the serenity on her face melted my last ounce of resistance. "I think Otto would have liked that. He was so good with people and had so many, many friends."

She stopped speaking and stared at me. Those light brown eyes seemed to plead with me.

She had me, and I think she knew it. "Of

course I'll go," I said.

"I want this to be a big, big event."

She had no idea what a big event it would be. How could she have known that someone would take her life in the beautiful, frozen land at the bottom of the world?

4

Twila had made the travel arrangements for all of us. I didn't want to calculate what it must have cost her. She had booked forty-seven seats on a Delta flight to Buenos Aires. We all met on the E Concourse at the Hartsfield-Jackson Airport in Atlanta. Everyone arrived at least two hours before our flight. Betty Freeman later told me she was so afraid of being late that she had arrived nearly four hours early. Even two hours seemed a little extreme to me, but that's what the airlines suggested.

That meant I had two hours to avoid eye contact with Burton. I saw him, and I'm sure he saw me. It was almost like a dance routine. I moved in one direction, and he moved in the opposite. Although I was conscious of his presence and location every minute of the two hours, I successfully avoided eye contact with him.

To his credit, he made no move to come

26

near me. I tried to observe him by looking at reflections in the glass windows or glancing at him from behind. I did have a feeling that he might be doing the same thing, but I restrained myself from trying to catch him at it. My emotions were still raw, and I didn't want any contact with him.

Heather Wilson, who knew we had dated, came over to me. "You and the pastor aren't with each other."

"You're very observant," I said in what I considered a noncommittal way.

"What's with you and Burton?"

"Nothing is what's with Burton and me."

"You know what I mean."

"We no longer date."

"Oh, that's wonderful! I mean, that's probably terrible or something for you." She smiled. "Did he cast you aside?"

"Ask him."

"So he's available, is he?"

"Ask him," I repeated and walked away.

She definitely wasn't Burton's type even though she was a lot prettier than I am. She's also six inches shorter and looks good when she stands next to him. She could wear heels and still look good beside him.

All right, she was gorgeous — one of the prettiest women I'd ever seen. Her features were flawless — alabaster skin, full red lips, patrician nose, and blue eyes. Her thick black hair was pulled back in a severe bun, which would have detracted from any other woman's appearance but only enhanced hers. Heather wore a richly textured sapphire blue dress that probably cost more than I spend on clothes in a year.

Our brochure advised us to wear warm, casual clothes for the trip. At the airport the rest of us wore leisure clothes (that is, mostly jeans or warm-up suits). I wore flat shoes. I told myself it was because heels were totally out of place on such a trip — which they were — but it also brought my height down so that I was less than an inch taller than Burton — I mean, if we ever stood next to each other again.

When Heather spoke to Burton, she got close to him — a little closer than most people would. But then, Heather would never win an award for being subtle.

Until they called us to board, we moved around in small groups. Our group made up almost half of the passengers on the Delta flight.

Twila and I sat together near the rear of the plane, so we were able to board before Burton. That avoided an awkward moment for me. We left on time, which was just after midnight. It was a ten-hour flight to Buenos

Aires, and we landed around ten o'clock the next morning. We were still in the same time zone, so we didn't have to worry about changing our watches.

We landed at Buenos Aires only about half an hour late. Going through Immigration was simple enough. We collected our luggage. I smirked when I saw the huge suitcase that Heather pulled. I overheard someone say that she had paid forty-nine dollars because she was above the seventy-pound weight limit.

We met together just outside Immigration. Twila had arranged for us to eat at a restaurant in the airport. I noticed with chagrin that somehow Heather had gotten Burton to pull her monstrous-sized suitcase. He traveled with one large carryall.

After our meal together, a fleet of taxis took us to the domestic airport, where we boarded a LAPA plane that flew the whole way along the spectacular Atlantic coast. Three hours later we landed at Ushuaia, Tierra del Fuego, Argentina. Ushuaia is touted as the southernmost city in the world. It's at the tip of the Andes where Chile and Argentina meet and nestles between what the tourist books call the "spectacular snowcapped mountains of the Andes and the Beagle Channel." This is one time the brochures didn't exaggerate.

From the airport, again a fleet of taxis (actually six drivers who made repeated round trips) drove us to the edge of the town, turned onto a dirt road, and wound around a bluff that overlooked the ocean. Twila had booked most of our group at the Los Niros hotel — a remote and scenic spot, high over Ushuaia. It was too small for all of us, so she reserved rooms for fifteen people at another local hotel.

We learned that the niros is a tree. I spotted *one* in front of the hotel, and the clerk proudly acknowledged, "Yes, it is our most famous tree." As far as I could tell, it was also the most infamous. With no competition, they could say anything they wanted about it. The niros stood about twelve feet tall. It was scraggly and ugly, and I suppose the only type of tree strong enough to survive the harshness of the weather. Relentless winds shook the building constantly. Despite the sun and moderate temperatures (according to the thermometer it was almost forty degrees Fahrenheit), the harsh, blustery winds brought the windchill factor to slightly above zero.

After we checked in, I felt restless. I wrapped myself in two heavy knit sweaters and two pairs of slacks. I debated about whether to unpack my heavy gloves and knit cap. I decided it was too much effort. I was still tired from disrupted sleep on the plane. Any further delay inside my room, and I probably would have been forced to lie down and rest.

I went outside. On one side of our hotel, I gazed at the Andes and the country of Chile. On the other side, I marveled at the high waves of the ocean whipped up by persistent and unyielding winds that also ripped at my face. I couldn't decide which side was more beautiful.

The wind never let up. It was cold — the kind that seems to penetrate every layer of clothing. There was no snow, only wind. Later I walked into a low-lying area, much like a small valley. To my surprise, I actually saw a copse of trees. Just for fun, I counted them. There were eight. One of them would have measured more than eight feet high if it had been able to stand erect. Even there, the wind was so severe that they were permanently bowed.

Twenty minutes later my cold feet and numb hands told me it was time to go back to the Los Niros.

I spotted Burton with someone about two hundred feet ahead of me. They were obviously walking together into Ushuaia. I didn't have to guess the identity of the other person. Heather was appropriately dressed in what looked like wool pants and a parka. She has a very distinctive walk, and I wonder if *sashay* is the proper description. She also wore distinctive, fur-lined boots with three-inch heels. As always, she looked gorgeous.

Doesn't she ever look normal like the rest of us?

"What do you care?" I answered myself.

She's a shameless flirt.

"Right, Julie. What's the saying? It takes one to know one."

He's no longer my concern.

"That's right!" I said. Okay, I shouted it. He was no longer a part of my life. But my tear-filled eyes wouldn't let me lie to myself.

I went back into the hotel. I felt lonelier than I had in years. I wasn't sure why. Twila was my friend and there were others I liked to be around, but my heart was out there, wishing I were next to Burton.

From inside, I peeked back. I'm sure he didn't see me. Heather clung, but to his credit, Burton seemed indifferent to her. His head was bowed slightly forward to brace against the torturous wind. It seemed as if she talked constantly. If he answered her, it wasn't with much animation.

You're through with Burton. Remember?

I turned and walked toward the dining room. It was closed, but when I waved a dollar bill, a nice waiter smiled at me — or maybe he smiled at the money in my hand. "Tea? Chai? Te?"

With a full grin he led me to a small alcove where I found hot water and tea bags. After handing him the dollar, hearing his cheery thanks, and retorting, *"De nada,"* I made myself a cup of tea, went back into the fairly small lobby, sat in the corner, and began to read.

All right, I didn't read, but I had an open book. And yes, I glanced out the window occasionally — like every eight seconds. More than an hour passed before Burton and Heather came back. She pretended to trip and grabbed his arm. Such a cheap trick.

But then, I had used the same trick the first time Burton and I walked together at Palm Island.

But of course, that was different.

As I sat alone, a terrible sense of foreboding crept over me. I kept pushing it aside, trying to convince myself that it was my anxiety about Burton.

Afterward, I wondered if I had done something — anything — or just paid attention to the nagging sense of dread that came over me, would I have been able to save Twila's life?

5

I turned away when Burton and Heather walked into the hotel. I stayed in the lobby nursing my long-cold cup of tea until it was time for dinner.

I called Twila, but she didn't feel like going to the dining room. She had already arranged for her meal to be brought to her room. She assured me that her medication took care of any pain. "I'm tired, my dear, just tired." She went to bed. I was in the room next to hers with a connecting door. I wanted to leave it open in case she needed me. Twila wouldn't allow it.

When I reached the dining hall, I sat down near Betty Freeman and Shirley Brackett (who was at the table without her brother, Frank). When I asked about him, she said, "He's tired and is having his dinner in his room."

The two women chatted constantly. I smiled and made brilliant comments such as "Oh," or "Hmm." They didn't seem to notice that I didn't talk.

That inner nagging wouldn't let up.

I tried not to notice Burton come into the dining room. He hurried past me and sat with Thomas Tomlinson, Mickey Brewer, and a half-dozen people I didn't know. Less than a minute later, Heather pranced into the room. Okay, *pranced* is my prejudiced word. I'll try it again. Heather entered the room as only Heather can. I didn't see where she went (my back was to Burton and the others), but I heard her say, "Oh, I should have been here earlier. I would have loved to sit with you."

No gallant man offered to give up his seat — or so I assume — because she came back and took the only empty space at our table.

The next morning after breakfast, we were told we could explore the town, but we were to meet in front of the Albatross Hotel no later than four o'clock, and we would be transported to the dock from there. They assured us the hotel was easy to find.

After breakfast, Twila and I wandered around Ushuaia for a couple of hours. For me, it was the most desolate place I had ever seen or imagined. The rugged spine of the Andes met the sea at the southern tips of Chile and Argentina. We learned Ushuaia had originally been a penal colony and about forty thousand people lived there.

Twila and I and ten others signed up for a half-day tour of Parque Nacional Park in Tierra del Fuego, which abuts the Chilean border. It was the only tour we could take, because the ship left at four thirty. We rode in a van with a guide named Nora. Although she was pretty and friendly, her English was marginal. She answered every question, but most of the time, her answers had little relevance to what we asked.

At four o'clock we were at the hotel. As I stepped out of the tour bus, Burton stood right there. There was about a three-foot space from the lower step to the ground. He held out a hand to each female passenger.

I stared into those blue eyes for a fraction of a second before I looked away. "Thank you," I mumbled. Because I looked away, I stumbled — accidentally — and he grabbed me.

"I think I've done this before," he said softly.

"Oh, really?" I hurriedly moved on. I love it when I can say something like that. Too late I remembered that was part of what Burton liked about me.

From then until the bus arrived, which

was nearly half an hour later, I kept my back to him. That wasn't easy. He moved around and talked to various people — he's quite outgoing that way.

He chatted for a minute or two with Twila, but I still kept my back to him. *Take that,* I thought. *I won't look into those gorgeous blue eyes. I won't let your dazzling smile get to me.*

He walked away and spoke with the next group. The bus finally arrived. I had to laugh. We could see the dock from where we stood. We boarded a bus and rode less than half a mile to where we were to embark. Our ship, the *Vaschenko,* was scheduled to leave port at 4:30 p.m., or as they called it, 1630 hours.

The summer season was nearing its end, although there were still almost fifteen hours of sunlight. By March, no ships would leave the area of Patagonia until after the sun appeared again well above the horizon. Someone said that would be August, but I knew there would be no cruise ships until November.

I had been on Caribbean cruises twice and had enjoyed the luxury and the size of the huge ocean liners. Perhaps I expected something like that, but the *Vaschenko* seemed tiny, like something out of a 1930s black-and-white movie. No luxury here, but it looked sturdy, and I liked the warm smile of the captain.

Sunil Robert, the captain, greeted each of us as we boarded. He held a chart and personally checked off each name and told us the location of our cabins. Even if I hadn't been able to tell from Captain Robert's dark skin and straight black hair, I would have known he was from India by his delightful accent. He spoke English well, with an accent that fluctuated between British English and East Indian.

Not that I paid much attention, but he was quite handsome, about thirty-five, and just under six feet tall, with a stocky build that had just begun to turn soft around the midsection. As we got closer, I observed his wedding ring, which made him suddenly seem less attractive.

He smiled and shook my hand, and it was a warm, firm handshake. He told me that I was in cabin six, and my roommate was Betty Freeman. (I already knew that, of course.)

I went to my cabin and saw that my luggage was already in place and on the bunk nearer the door, so I decided that was mine. My bunk bed resembled something I had slept on during summer camp, except that this one was much sturdier and bolted to the floor. The room had one window, but we were right at sea level, so I saw nothing but water spraying against the heavily paned porthole. Each of us had a cupboard. One-half was shelving and the other for hanging. On the top shelf was a life vest with instructions that we were always to have it on when we left the ship. In one corner was a small desk, a chair, and a reading lamp. I have no idea why they called it a reading lamp. It had about twenty-five watts of light. The overhead light was just about bright enough so I could read. The toilet was outside our door on our left with the shower on the right. The ship had two dining rooms, each seating about twenty-five people.

The ship pulled out exactly at four thirty. Most of us scurried to the top and watched the ship navigate through the generally calm waters of the Beagle Channel. I went to my cabin, unpacked, and then explored the ship. Because of its modest size, that didn't take long. This was no Carnival ship, and we had no casino, restaurant, disco, stage, swimming pool, shops, TV, newspapers, or any outside communication. This was exactly what we had expected.

Betty Freeman and I shared the bathroom with the occupants of four other cabins —

but we were the closest. We never had anywhere to go except the dining room on our floor, the lecture room down one flight, the bar up one flight, or the navigation bridge. To get alone during the days at sea, I realized there would be only one place to go: I walked up to the top deck, where the wind whipped me from all directions. Shivering with cold and occasionally facing pelting snow, I walked. I would rarely have company.

Twila chose the Amundsen Suite for herself — the one luxury cabin on the entire ship and at a cost of slightly under $8,000. That kind of luxury wasn't typical of Twila, but I understood the reason.

I had agreed to meet Twila twenty minutes later so we could watch the ship move out of the dock. It would have been uneventful except that several dusky dolphins followed us.

Twila loved the movement and the noise and the cold and the wind. I let her enjoy it. I watched her carefully. She insisted she was in no pain and told me in her firm-but-nice voice, "I did not bring you to be my nurse."

I apologized, but I didn't stop watching after her.

I wish I had watched more closely.

6

We had tea about five thirty while we listened to all the announcements and ended with a lifeboat drill. We had to report on the deck with life vests. We lined up in two rows. I paid no attention to anyone around us, but as I put on my life vest, I must have taken a step backward and somehow lost my balance. Strong arms grabbed my shoulders.

"Easy."

"Thank you," I said without turning around. I knew who stood behind me.

I heard none of the lecture, because I wondered if Burton focused on me or if he noticed that I had cut my hair shorter. Why should he notice?

Do you really care? I asked myself.

I chose not to answer my own question.

Instead, I asked myself, *Am I destined to run into Burton like this for the entire cruise?* One of my colleagues at the mental health center always insisted that we unconsciously attract what we want — good or bad. I hoped she was wrong.

The drill finally over, I stepped forward. Betty had brought along a small bag and dropped it at her feet (although we had been told to bring nothing). In my haste to get away from Burton, I tripped over the bag and started to plunge forward.

Strong arms grabbed me in midfall.

"You're good at falling," the voice said. "This is the best fall you've done since we met on Palm Island."

"That time it was deliberate," I said before I could stop myself.

"I know," he said and chuckled.

I made it a habit to get to the dining room early — earlier than Burton. The dining room was really two rooms, separated by a wall. The passageway led directly to the left dining room, and we had to walk a few feet to enter the room on the right. I went there where it was less crowded.

To his credit, Burton sat in the other room. I wondered why.

I must be crazy, I thought. *I don't want him around me and I don't want to talk to him, yet if he doesn't show up, I feel slighted.*

I sighed and thought about what I'd say

to a client. I'd say it more diplomatically, but in essence, my message would be, "Get over him."

That's what I'll do, I thought.

I looked around the dining room. One cook was Russian and the other was Finnish. They came out before every evening meal and told us how wonderfully they had prepared for us. They stood in the doorway between the two rooms so everyone could see them.

Every midday and evening meal started with soup with exotic names and strange flavors, but I liked them all. We had a choice of meat, chicken, or vegetarian. Sometimes fish replaced meat. We selected our choices at breakfast by checking a posted list. Simple enough.

The meals on the ship were excellent. We had choices of two entrées at lunch and three at dinner, and could have seconds if we wanted. Even for the five vegetarians the chef always came through — although I wouldn't attempt to explain some of the odd combinations. We later marveled that we still had fresh lettuce and only moderately ripe bananas on the last day at sea when there were no places along the way to get provisions. The cooks had developed a system to keep fresh produce stored in such a way that it didn't ripen too quickly.

It was easier to focus on ripe bananas than to wonder what was going on inside Burton's head.

"Stop it!" I told myself.

I wished I could obey my commands as well as I could throw them out.

Around midnight on our first night, we entered the open sea. We had heard about the dreaded Drake Passage that separates South America from Antarctica and had been told it is the roughest sea in the world. After we went through the passage, I don't think any of us doubted the accuracy of that statement. I slept fairly well that night because once the ride became bumpy, I packed clothes and luggage around my body and lay in the shape of a banana. I didn't get knocked around very much. Many passengers wore ear patches or took Phenergan for motion sickness — and I'm not sure they did much good. The next day I heard from at least two people that they had received shots for motion sickness. The ship rocked so hard that at times most of us felt as if we were being tossed from a horizontal position to a ninety-degree angle in our beds. The doctor had given me a few Phenergan tablets in case I needed them. I didn't.

45

I loved showering the next morning. I held on to a steel wall post with one hand while I washed with the other. It was impossible to walk across the small cabin (perhaps eight feet by twelve) without holding on. Maneuvering the short hallways tested our walking ability. As long as we held on to the railings, we were all right.

Few passengers showed up at breakfast. Other than seasickness, nothing exciting happened the first three days as we went across the Drake Passage. If we wanted to go outside, we could see any number of albatross, especially the magnificent wandering albatross and the southern giant petrels. Mickey Brewer spotted two minke whales and Donny Otis yelled when he saw a humpback. I raced to the spots, but they just looked like big globs of brown or gray in the water. It was cold, windy, and wet on the deck, so I spent most of my time on the bridge. It was an excellent lookout spot, and the captain or some excited passenger would point out the wildlife.

Our ship plowed through seas so rough that at times no one was allowed on deck. We had to hang on to tables or walls to keep from toppling over when we walked. All of us spent a lot of time in our bunks and slept a lot the first two days. I read two books during that rough travel — after I insisted on a larger bulb in the reading lamp.

One of the crew members lectured on "The Early Discovery and Exploration of the Frozen Continent." I found it fascinating, but fewer than thirty of us attended.

This is boring stuff, I know, but it's important to explain all of this — especially after we had our first two landings. That's when the cruise was no longer just an Antarctic trip.

We spotted land at the end of the third day. Almost everyone raced up to the decks. I started up and discovered Burton just ahead of me. I turned and went back to my cabin. I'd see a lot of land soon.

The next day, before we made the first landing, Captain Robert briefed us on the dos and don'ts of Antarctica. By international agreement, the continent must remain undeveloped, with no damage to ecosystems. For example, visitors must haul out their own trash. We were not to touch any animals or come close enough to make them wary or fearful.

It became quite a task for me to avoid Burton. He didn't stalk me — he isn't the type — but he seemed to be around no matter where I went on the ship and when we landed.

Or was my colleague correct that I sent invisible vibes through the atmosphere to attract him? I usually laughed when she talked that way. Now I wondered.

A few hours later, we received an announcement about twenty minutes before the first of four motorized rubber rafts (called Zodiacs) left the ship. That was our signal to put on our heavy "landing clothes" as I called them. The captain also told us of weather conditions — no matter how he stated his report, it was always cold.

We had instructions on how to get into the Zodiacs, which were large, heavy-duty inflatables with flat bottoms that allowed them to land directly onto the cobble and ice-strewn beaches.

The first time I held back until Burton had gotten into a Zodiac and it had shoved off. To be honest, it was stressful. If only I'd felt indifferent to him or hated him, I wouldn't have been so stressed over seeing him. Each time our eyes met, I looked away and wished I had not come along on the cruise.

I lined up for the next Zodiac. We had to have both hands free to get on and off. We women left our purses and personal items on the ship. Those with cameras slung them over their shoulders or, if they were small enough, tucked them inside their enormous parkas. We were told to step carefully and quickly from the launching platform and to accept the assistance offered by the crew. We were not to hold the helper's hand but instead to use the sailor's grip (grab each other by the forearm). Heather complained that she thought the forearm was "a most unattractive place to grab."

I thought of two or three rude comments, but I kept my mouth shut.

Most of the time (to my surprise), the temperatures stayed slightly below freezing, but with the winds, who would have known? I would have guessed about fifty degrees below zero, but Jon Friesen teased me and said I must have no blood flowing through my body.

"How can it flow when it's already frozen?" I asked.

"Maybe I need to warm you up."

He was smiling, but he just wasn't my type. I said, "A hot shower after our return will work better." I moved away from him.

Twila had even taken care of the biggest clothing problems. She had personally bought a blue rain suit of coated nylon for each of us (after we gave her our sizes). We put them over our clothing and they kept us dry, protected us from the wind, and also gave some amount of warmth. She also bought us heavy rubber boots — two sizes larger than our regular shoes so we could pad them with as many extra socks as we wanted — or so they said. They were slightly more than a foot high and had strong, ridged nonskid soles, which we needed for landings on rocks or ice. Each time we went ashore, I decided I would wear three pairs of heavy wool socks — that was as many as I could get inside the boots.

I brought polypropylene underwear because it keeps the body warm without adding bulk. On top of that I wore a heavy turtleneck and a hooded fleece jacket. Keeping the hands warm and dry, the brochure we received told us, was often a problem. I brought two pairs of thin polypropylene glove liners to wear under my wool gloves.

We lined up in our dorky gear on deck and laughed at how outrageous we looked. Several of the women commented on how fat it made them appear, including Heather Wilson, but I reminded her, "Honey, when they can choose between you and penguins on the white continent, they won't even notice what you're wearing."

They were all wet landings. That is, we had no piers, and our Zodiac pulled up fairly close but not close enough. Our driver jumped out and stood in water about eight inches deep. He offered us a grip to climb out. From there we waded to shore in freezing-but-shallow water.

Here's how the system worked: Four Zodiacs carried twelve passengers ashore, which was a ride of less than five minutes from the ship.

The landing at King George Island in the early afternoon was set up quite efficiently. Although Twila wasn't murdered on the first landing, it's important for me to tell you about it. The murderer — as we realized later — figured out the system and planned to kill her at a subsequent landing. Had it not been for a careful and observant captain, Twila's death might have gone undetected. No one might ever have known what had happened to her.

7

To go ashore, we lined up at the side of the ship to get into the Zodiacs. We first had to pass by what the captain called the "landing tag board." That was the most important and the first of two ways to keep track of passengers. The murderer must have taken careful note of the procedure.

Each of us had a number — assigned to us at random as far as I could see. When we left the ship, the tag faced right and we picked it up, turned it to the left, and put it back. The tag was nothing but a piece of wood with a number in bright yellow and a hole to put it on the hooks on the board. The captain checked the landing tag board before the last Zodiac left. If there were any keys on the board facing right, he either had been told the person was sick, which usually meant seasick, or someone had chosen not to go. Of course, anyone could choose not to go, but no one opted for that the first two landings.

We had to line up wearing our life jackets. The life jackets were the second way to keep track of us. After we waded through the shallow water, a few feet from the shore we were supposed to take off the life jackets and drop them on the ground (in a dry spot). A few of the people didn't bother to drop off their life jackets but wore them when they walked around.

That was the second thing that almost made Twila's death go undetected.

When we got ready to go back to the ship, we picked up a life jacket. The point of leaving and taking up life jackets was that if the number of people who left to go back to the ship was correct, when we left, there would be no life jackets on the ground.

We could switch to another Zodiac on the return. In that case, we were supposed to notify the driver and were responsible to have a life jacket on when we boarded the Zodiac. Occasionally someone came in, say, the first Zodiac and, instead of going back with that group, walked around and went back with the third or fourth Zodiac.

The fourth Zodiac would not leave un-less every life jacket had been picked up off the beach. That's why the killer had to understand the second part of the counting system.

The azure blueness of the sky overwhelmed me. I had never seen such a vivid color before. We spotted large icebergs of many shapes and hues. Some were bluish (the darker the blue, the older the glacier they had broken off from). Others had tunnel-like holes through them, or they appeared to have turned upside down. A few resembled mushrooms. One passenger said, "This is a veritable Rorschach test in white and 3-D."

On King George Island, we had our first look — and smell — of Antarctica. The odor of penguin guano overpowered me for a minute, but I soon became accustomed to that and to the two-inch thickness of it on the ground as I walked around.

The air felt so fresh, I stopped several times and breathed deeply. The cold nipped at my toes, but I kept moving and wriggling them as I walked. Clouds lined the horizon as if to signal bad weather in the hours ahead. During the two hours or so we stayed on King George Island, the wind increased considerably.

I could only say again and again that it was the most spectacular place imaginable.

This was one trip when pictures hardly did justice to reality. Hundreds of penguins, dozens of Weddell seals, two leopard seals, and two fur seals seemed totally at home in the rocky landscape of the desolate wasteland. We gazed at a huge glacier farther down the beach, and several of us hiked over to it. We didn't go far, because the captain warned us that calving action (breaking off) could happen without warning, and it would sweep us into the ocean.

As I walked along, I took out my brochure to identify the species of penguins. Five of the seventeen existing varieties lived there, and that day (for the first and only time) I was able to see all of them on the same island: gentoo, Adélie, macaroni, rockhopper, and chinstrap. The penguins, sometimes called wingless birds, fascinated most of us. We could watch them, seemingly endlessly, without getting bored.

Penguins have many humanlike mannerisms and portly body shapes. If we moved slowly, we could get within a few feet of them. They were afraid only of fast movements, because birds of prey sometimes swept down and snatched their babies or stole their eggs.

It amazed me to be able to stand so near and watch these birds climb a steep, slippery hill. Sometimes they fell backward, but they just started again. Yet when those awkward creatures swam, a transformation took place. They flipped into the air, arched their bodies, and, porpoiselike, dove hundreds of feet into the ocean to catch fish. They endured temperatures of minus seventy degrees. We learned in one of our lectures that males share the job of sitting on the unhatched eggs and also feed the chicks by regurgitating food through their beaks for the babies to suck out. Females usually have two eggs. In years when the fish supply is low, they feed one chick and push away the other, which eventually dies.

After two hours ashore, we returned to the ship to set sail for our next landing.

As soon as we returned to the ship, we partnered with one or two others to hose down our boots that were packed thick with penguin droppings.

The captain said it delicately. "Wash your boots carefully after each landing to avoid accidentally transporting seeds or other organisms from landing site to landing site. Your cabin mate and the stewardesses will also appreciate it."

The system was simple; it was also efficient. After all the Zodiacs returned to the ship, the captain checked to make sure that all the tags had been turned back to their original position.

As far as I know, no one counted life jackets on the return to the ship. As long as none remained on the beach, there was no need to count.

That was the mistake.

The waters roiled again, and that night was as bad as the first one. This time the wave action was head to toe, producing roller-coaster sensations, whereas the first night it had been side to side. That's the description the other passengers gave me — I don't know; I slept extremely well.

Captain Robert had scheduled our second landing to be at Brown Bluff, on the northern tip of the Antarctic continent. The Zodiac trips were a bit rougher this time, and the huge waves sprayed us as we made our way to shore. Jeff Adams said his camera froze, so he bribed two of the other passengers to share pictures with him after the trip.

Before we left for our Brown Bluff landing, Captain Robert lectured us about a 1902 Norwegian expedition that rivaled Shackleton's for harrowing drama. The men endured two winters at Brown Bluff. After two years and various rescue attempts, two parties independently arrived from different directions on the same day to save them.

By then, we had already landed once, and everyone understood the routine. We felt like veterans of the Antarctic; no crew member had to remind us what to do. The killer must have counted on that fact.

I suppose that sense of rhythm and routine lulled my protective senses. I spent most of my time alone when we landed at Brown Bluff. It was more than avoiding Burton. I continually questioned myself, and I had to be alone to do that.

I loved Burton — I couldn't get away from that reality. But I couldn't marry him, knowing what I did about him.

If only he would confess — I stopped myself right there. I'd argued that one with myself only about 912 times.

In exhaustion, I would remind myself of one thing: It wasn't my choice; the decision was Burton's.

8

The Brown Bluff landing fascinated me. Besides the remains of the 1902 expedition's shack made of rock walls about three feet high, penguins were everywhere. While we walked among the birds, the winds increased considerably. *Cold* hardly describes the effect. My teeth chattered and my fingers became numb, even though I wore thick gloves and my two pairs of liners.

Two of the Zodiacs had returned by the time the weather deteriorated, but no one hurried back to the third and fourth ones. That implied that everyone left was determined to see the wildlife. The wind soon calmed, and I was glad we had stayed.

I marveled at the vast numbers of penguins and seals. Perhaps twenty minutes later, without warning, a stiff wind again battered us, followed by hard-pounding snow. And I mean hard — the snow felt like rock granules sandblasting my face. I'd take maybe five steps with my eyes closed, open them quickly for a step, and then shut them again. Other than the Zodiac staff, who wore goggles, none of us could see much of anything.

I raced for the third Zodiac. At least six people were ahead of me, and others hurried behind me. Our driver helped the twelfth and last passenger in, and we headed back toward the ship.

The waves utterly drenched us. Despite our rain-repellent clothes, the water got to all of us. The trip back to the ship seemed to take longer than the trip to land, and the weather continued to deteriorate. The wind had subtly blown us somewhat adrift from the ship, and I think our Zodiac driver was lost for a few minutes. He didn't say so, but the wariness of his normally calm face gave him away.

When he grinned, I relaxed. I knew he had spotted the ship.

We got aboard the *Vaschenko* and hurried through the boot-washing process as quickly as we could. My hands were almost numb.

Just as I started to go inside, I saw the fourth Zodiac tie up.

I didn't look at faces or count the number of people aboard.

That was a mistake.

■ ■ ■ ■

Captain Robert canceled the scheduled landing for that afternoon. He said that if the weather permitted, we would land at Paulet Island the next day.

The storm didn't abate for the rest of the day, but I felt incredibly lucky to have enjoyed the spectacular view on Brown Bluff.

Once we were all on board, the captain carefully checked the tag board, just as he did at the end of every reboarding process throughout the trip.

"Everyone has made it back," he said and smiled. He had also done that on the previous landing.

About half an hour after each landing, we had tea in the dining room. It was much like the English tea with a variety of small sandwiches, sweets, tea, coffee, and hot chocolate.

After our return from Brown Bluff, the ship pulled anchor and started on the next leg of our trip. As we sat drinking our tea, I realized I hadn't seen Twila. We weren't on the same Zodiac going out, and I hadn't seen her on the island. Unless we were fairly close, it was next to impossible to recognize each other because we all looked alike when we wore our special "uniforms."

"Where's Twila?" I called out. "Anyone seen her?"

"Yes, she was on our Zodiac going over," Betty said. "We were the last ones to leave."

"Yeah, that's right," someone else said. "I remember now."

"What about coming back?" I asked.

"I assume she was with us," Betty said. "I didn't count —"

"There was no one left on the island," Pat Borders said. Pat was a real estate broker who attended Burton's church.

I wondered if she had gotten sick on the return trip. I asked, but no one seemed to remember. They were so busy taking pictures of icebergs, penguins, skuas, and seals that no one paid attention to other passengers.

"That's odd that she's not down here," I said. "Perhaps she's not well." I excused myself and left the dining room. *Oh no, I* thought, *the cancer. She said there would be no pain. Maybe she was wrong.*

"May I go with you?"

Without turning around, I knew Burton's voice. I didn't want to be alone with him, even to walk up two flights of steps with

62

him. "I'd prefer to go alone." I hoped he caught the frosty tone in my voice. I'm good at frosty tones.

I knocked on Twila's cabin door, but there was no answer. None of the rooms had locks on them, so I pushed the door open. Her room was empty. She had reserved a private room, and it was truly luxury quality — with a double bed, two lamps, and a large closet.

"Maybe she's up on the navigation bridge," I said aloud to myself. We were welcome there at any time. They had three or four chairs so we could sit and get a marvelous view or simply stand at the window that stretched the full width of the room.

I walked up the final flight of steps and entered the bridge. The captain and two other officers were there.

No Twila.

I left abruptly and hurried to the lounge and the theater-lecture room where we watched films and the staff lectured on the days when we were unable to land.

I opened the door to what we called the sick bay, but it was empty. I braved the freezing wind and took a few steps on the deck to make sure she wasn't there. I knew it was useless, because no one would have been able to stand on the deck at that time. The snow had stopped, but the wind hadn't decreased.

I rushed back to the bridge and approached Captain Robert. "Excuse me," I said, "this may be nothing, but Twila Belk doesn't seem to be around."

He said nothing but gave me a skeptical look as if to ask, "How can that be possible?"

I explained that no one had seen her on the Zodiac for the return trip.

"There must be a mistake," the captain said with his thick Indian accent. "All tags have been turned back. No life jackets were left on Brown Bluff."

"I've been everywhere on the ship except for the others' cabins. They're all having tea, so I'm sure she's not in any of them."

He sent someone to the lounge and someone else to the theater.

I went back to the dining room. "Has anyone seen Twila?"

No one spoke.

"She has to be around," Pat Borders said. "On a ship this small —"

I cut him off and walked away. I went back to Twila's room, and I didn't find her. I was frantic. Even though I knew that the weather on the deck was too bad for any of us, I searched again. Was it possible that she had walked out there, felt weak, fainted, and been swept overboard? I took three steps out the door and let my gaze sweep slowly over the entire deck from the starboard side. I went to the other side of the ship and did the same thing from that door. No one. A fine skin of undisturbed snow covered the deck, so it was obvious no one had been there.

I went back to the dining room. As far as I could tell, no one had moved. No one seemed concerned. Jeff told a funny story about his trip to Alaska, and as soon as he finished, Jon had one about being lost in Bhutan.

I poured myself a cup of tea and sat alone. *Where is she? Where could she disappear to on a small ship like this?*

Twenty minutes later, most of us had finished our tea and were ready to go to our rooms to read or nap. The captain walked into the dining room. Behind him came Ivan, a tall, blond, Swedish-looking man, who claimed to be a Russian from Kiev.

"One minute, please," the captain said. "We have a problem here. We are missing one passenger."

"Twila? Where is Twila?" Betty called out. "Is she sick or — ?"

"She is not aboard the ship," the captain said.

9

Everyone seemed to talk at once. The captain finally raised his voice. "Please be seated, everyone. We need to be quite clear about whatever has happened."

I had already told him that Twila had gone over to Brown Bluff with the fourth group. "Those of you who left on the fourth Zodiac," he said, "please to raise your hands." He counted eleven.

"On the Zodiac trip across to Brown Bluff, who was near Mrs. Belk?"

They talked among themselves, and Pat said, "I think she was on my right. You know, we have different groups each time, and —"

"Yes, I know, but of course," the captain said.

"Who was on the other side of her?" He grabbed a sheet of paper from the bulletin board and drew a rough sketch of a Zodiac. "The engine was here," he said. "Ivan drove the fourth Zodiac." He held it up and asked the eleven people to come forward and tell him where they stood on the way out. He said *stood* but the sides are rounded with ropes, and most people sat on the sides and held on to the ropes.

It took several minutes of discussion, but they finally agreed that Twila had been seated between Pat Borders and Jeff Adams, an elder in Burton's church.

"Very good," the captain said. He turned the paper over, drew another crude picture, and said, "We shall now see where you stood on the return trip."

"I — I was on another Zodiac," Jon said. "My stomach was heaving a little, and I wanted to get back."

"You are all right now, are you?"

"Not wonderful, but I'm okay," he said. "That is, after I vomited twice."

"I am sorry —"

"So I decided to go on the other Zodiac. They were getting into the boat right then. I sent word to Ivan that —"

"You did not tell him yourself? You told someone else?"

"Certainly," Jon said. "I was too miserable."

I watched him for some sign to show that he was lying. I saw nothing.

"To whom did you speak, sir?"

"I don't know. I don't remember. I felt too miserable to pay attention. Someone was walking toward Ivan's boat. I grabbed his arm — or it may have been a woman — and said, "I'm sick. I'll go back on this Zodiac. Tell Ivan.""

"Then what happened?"

"I climbed into the Zodiac and said, 'I'm sick. I'm going back early.' I leaned over the side of the boat and barfed. That was the first time. It happened again before we reached the ship."

"Can someone verify this?"

"Oh yeah, all of us on boat three can," one of the men said.

The captain turned to Ivan. "How many people were on your Zodiac on the return?"

"Ten, sir."

"But you went out with twelve."

"Yes, sir, but someone told me that two of them had become —" He spoke with a heavy accent, and it was obvious he searched for the correct word. "Sickness — two of them had become sickness and would have make their return on the third Zodiac."

"Who told you?"

"I do not remember, sir. I was speaking to you on the VHF radio." He dropped his head, unable to look at the captain. "Someone — and who it was I do not know — said to me, 'Two of them have return the other boat.' "

"Did the person explain?"

"Yes, sickness."

"Sick. Two people sick? Is that what the person said?"

"Yes, sick. That is the word. Yes, sir."

"Two of them?"

"Yes, Captain."

"You are sure?"

"Most absolutely."

"You have no idea who spoke to you?"

"Sir, on this voyage, everyone in this group wears the same, do they not? So I could not be to know. The wind blow heavy, snow fall. They come, all of them from forward to the Zodiac with their heads."

"Bent forward? Lowered?"

"Yes, Captain, that is what I meant."

The captain was obviously displeased at the lack of precise information, but Ivan added in a defensive tone, "I had but not yet finished speaking on the VHF radio to you, sir. And, sir, I was upset because —"

"Yes, I see," the captain said. He turned to the rest of us. "It was a small matter and not significant here. I had spoken some rather harsh words to Ivan about something quite unrelated to passengers."

We accepted that statement. Ivan hung his head while the captain talked, so we were all convinced that he had received a severe reprimand for something. He must have felt bad about the call then and even worse that he had not been attentive on the return.

The captain finally asked the obvious question: "Who gave the information to Ivan that two people would go on the other Zodiac?"

After a long silence, he said, "I see that we have no answer." He stared at us for a few seconds and made his next decision. One by one, Sunil Robert questioned all ten of the passengers on the fourth Zodiac. He asked Jon Friesen twice to tell him about being sick. There seemed no question about his vomiting.

As I listened, I thought he would make a good detective. He was obviously assured of himself and in control of the situation. Everyone seemed compliant.

Even after he had questioned the ten people, no one admitted talking to Ivan. No one noticed Jon get on the other Zodiac.

"Ivan just said something like, 'All here. Others on different boat,' " was the way Heather explained it.

"That's right," Donny Otis said and imitated Ivan's voice.

"I didn't notice anyone being gone and I didn't count," Betty Freeman said. "It was obvious that everyone else had left Brown Bluff, so we took off."

"But every tag faces the correct way, including hers," the captain said. "Her number was seven. The tag was turned to show that she went ashore. It now faces the correct way to say that she has returned."

"I've searched everywhere for her," I said.

"So have I," Burton said.

The captain stared at me and then at Burton. He said nothing, but both of us knew what he was thinking.

"Twila is still on the island," Captain Robert said.

10

"The weather will not permit a Zodiac to land, so we shall stay anchored until the conditions have improved enough for someone to go back," the captain said.

He turned abruptly and left the room. About an hour later, we could feel the ship make a turn. Four hours later, the weather calmed sufficiently and a Zodiac left the ship. It was nearly 10:30 p.m., but no one had gone to bed. Because of the many hours of daylight, it wouldn't be a problem to get back to the island and look for Twila.

"Surely she wasn't left on the island," Pat said as we stood on deck and watched Ivan and two others take the Zodiac. "Why would anyone want to stay behind? There's nothing there —"

"There must be some other explanation," Thomas Tomlinson said. He was a baritone in the choir, and for a long time he had been one of Twila's most devoted admirers. He was in his late thirties. He once told me that his family was unable to send him to college. "My family was always poor," he had said. "I had five siblings, and neither of my uneducated parents ever made much money from their jobs."

When Twila learned that he was an exceptional student, she paid his total college expenses. He had returned to Clayton County and taught math in the Jonesboro High School. Only two years earlier he had become the assistant principal and next year would become the principal.

He could never say enough kind words about Twila. "She would not allow me to repay her. She told me that if I were truly thankful, I would find someone like me who needed help." His eyes watered when he said that. "My wife and I have decided to pay tuition for two students each year."

Thomas walked over and stood beside me. "I don't understand," he said. "I'm sure no one was left. I stood on the shore, and I was the last one to get into the Zodiac. I thought it was such a sad, desolate place."

He stared at me as if begging me to tell him Twila was going to be all right. I touched his arm. "Pray. If she is alive, we'll find her."

"If?" he asked, and I thought I was going

to have to comfort him, but he turned around and sat down at the end of the table. He stared into space.

I walked over to the coffeepot, not because I wanted another cup but because I didn't want to hear the discussion among the other passengers. I knew they would continue to speculate, and it would end with something negative. I wasn't ready for that.

Twila is missing.

I wanted to cry, but I held back. *I knew.* That terrible sense of foreboding I had felt back at Ushuaia lodged inside my throat, and I felt as if I would have to vomit.

"Twila is missing," I said aloud to myself, because I wasn't quite ready to say the word *dead.*

That she was missing was the only fact I knew. As soon as that thought flashed into my mind, I wondered if she had taken her own life. Surely if that was her plan, she wouldn't have gone to the trouble of booking the cruise and paying our expenses. That kind of suicide would be incomprehensible.

No, not Twila. She was too strong a person and too committed a Christian to do such a thing.

But still.

Surely no one would harm her. I held a cup of tea in my hand, but my gaze shifted from person to person. I'm not sure what I expected to see, but no one had an appearance of guilt or remorse. I saw confusion on almost every face.

"I can't believe anything has happened to —," Betty said and started to sob.

"We don't know anything yet," Burton said. He wrapped an arm around her.

"Of course you're correct," she said, but her words didn't sound convincing.

As I half-listened, I thought again about Twila telling me she had cancer. On the plane she assured me that she experienced little pain and had sufficient medication to take care of it. "It will be a few months before the pain becomes acute," she said. "For now, you are not to be concerned."

She had turned her face from me and stared out the window. It was too dark to see anything, but I knew it was her way to say the discussion was closed.

No, Twila wouldn't take her own life.

But she was missing.

These people — all of us — loved her. We were her friends. I didn't know everybody, but I couldn't believe that any of them would do anything to harm Twila.

If it wasn't suicide, what other explanation could there be?

We heard the lowering of the anchor. I

76

wasn't sure, but I thought I heard another Zodiac leaving. Along with several others, I hurried to the launching door and watched it push away from the ship. I soon lost sight of the small motorized boat. It was impossible to see the land from where we were.

It was cold standing there, but I couldn't move. My body began to shake, and I didn't know if it was from the weather or from my sense of loss. Just then, someone wrapped a blanket around my shoulders. "Thank you," I said. I didn't turn around because I didn't care who it was.

I had been on the third Zodiac and remembered the desolation of the place. There was a small hillock — perhaps a rise of six or seven feet — but that was the only place that wasn't quite flat until we walked perhaps three hundred feet. After that, it was all steep, almost like mountains. It just didn't seem possible that anyone could have done Twila harm on Brown Bluff.

At that very moment, I knew what I had not been willing to say aloud: Twila was dead. I turned my back to everyone and tried to stand straight and tall, but tears slid slowly down my cheeks. I loved her. It shouldn't end like this for anyone. Especially not for Twila. I had never met anyone who exemplified the Christian life the way she did.

Just then a hand touched my left shoulder, and I knew who stood behind me. I didn't have the strength to resist him, but I didn't surrender. I stood as I was.

"I loved her, too," he whispered. "She's gone, isn't she?"

Without thinking, I twirled around and buried my face in Burton's shoulder.

This time the tears fell freely, and I couldn't hold back.

Several minutes passed, and I pulled away from Burton. "Please, please don't talk to me," I said.

Burton said nothing, but he didn't move.

I have no sense of how long we stood there, but I heard the Zodiac before I saw it. As soon as it got close enough, I spotted a blue-suited body lying flat on the floor. The hood was pulled so that I couldn't see the face. I didn't notice the life jacket beside her, but Burton later found out that they had discovered it next to her body.

"Someone killed her," Burton said.

His words threw me into convulsive sobs, but I didn't turn away. He tried to wrap his arms around me, but I pushed him away. "No! No! No!" I shouted.

By the time the Zodiac pulled alongside the ship, the captain was at the entrance and stepped in front of me. "Please return back to the dining room." He said *please,* but it was a command.

"She is — she was my best friend —"

"Please. Now."

Burton forced me to turn around. He wrapped his arms around me, and I didn't have the strength to resist. He kept his arms around me as he led me back to the dining room. Several others looked up as the small group of us walked into the room. I'm sure our faces told them the truth.

A hush came over the entire room.

Someone screamed.

"What happened?" Jon Friesen called out. "Did they find her?"

"How badly is she — ?" Heather asked. She had enough sense to stop in midsentence. "Oh no! Oh, Lord Jesus, no!"

I couldn't answer any of them. I sat down. Burton sat next to me, his arm still around me. I knew his arm was there, and I felt a strange kind of comfort at that moment. I didn't move until the captain joined us.

11

"Something has happened to Mrs. Belk," Sunil Robert said.

I looked into his eyes, waiting for him to tell us something more. I willed for him to say that she was only sick or badly hurt.

"A heart attack? On the island?" Betty Freeman asked. "Is that what it was?"

"She looked healthy to me," Donny Otis said.

There seemed to be a long pause as if the captain tried to make up his mind how much to say.

"Mrs. Belk is dead."

"But how — ?" Sue Downs cried out. "I can't —"

"She was stabbed."

He obviously didn't want to say more, but several people persisted. He finally admitted that as far as they could tell, she had been stabbed repeatedly in the neck. "She either died from the wounds or was left to die." He would say no more.

"Murdered?" Mickey Brewer said. Mickey owned the largest insurance agency in the county and was one of the church's most faithful ushers. "Not Twila! Not that wonderful, godly woman!"

"I'm not sure what procedures to follow," the captain said. "Already we have notified the American Embassy in Buenos Aires. As you will agree, the rest of the trip is canceled. We are returning to Argentina immediately."

"Aren't you going to search us?" someone behind me asked.

"I think not."

"But why not?"

"I seriously considered doing that very thing, but chose not to do so. First, we do not know what we're looking for except that it was some kind of instrument — likely a knife. Second, I believe it would be impossible to search every place on board. Third, on a ship like this, it would take little effort for someone to throw the weapon of death overboard unobserved."

"So it's possible the weapon has already gone into the ocean," Burton said.

"Yes, but of course, that is a strong possibility," the captain said.

"So what happens now?" Betty Freeman asked.

"We have already turned the ship around, and, as I said, we are on our way back to Buenos Aires."

We knew it would take two full days to get through the Drake Passage and back to the continent.

Several people asked questions — most of them out of shock. He answered none of them. He waited until the noise level had lessened. "I would like to talk to each passenger, one at a time."

"All the passengers?" someone asked.

"Yes. All."

He asked Burton to send in the passengers to see him one at a time. He went into the second, smaller dining room and sat down.

No one stayed in the room with him for more than three or four minutes. From the muted conversation, apparently he asked everyone essentially the same questions, such as "Which Zodiac did you take to Brown Bluff? To whom did you speak going across and coming back? What did you do on the island? Were you alone most of the time or with someone?"

When my turn came, I told him the truth: I had talked to no one either way. "Captain, I'm going through a difficult period right now," I said. "I recently broke up with a man — he's also a passenger. I came on the trip only because Twila is — was — my best friend and she begged me to."

"Precisely what did you do on the island?"

"I walked by myself," I said. "I wanted to get away from everyone. I needed to be where I could feel alone for a little while. I walked around and avoided everyone." Again I remembered the pelting snow. A few skua birds hovered around the penguins.

He asked me two or three more questions, and I know I answered them, but at that moment, I was so heavyhearted I don't remember what they were. I think he took notes, but I'm not sure.

As he got up, he said softly, "I am sorry for the loss of your special friend. No one has said a negative word about her, which makes this so strange. People do not murder those whom they love." He shook his head slowly. "Would they lie at a time like this?"

"I doubt that you'll find anyone to say an unkind word —" I stopped. "Of course, whoever killed her must have hated her."

"Yes, that must be so. Someone stabbed her — an act of great violence. That was no accident. It might have been done in a frenzy, but that I cannot say." He said he knew nothing about stabbing, so he couldn't say whether it was a large knife or what the person had used. Medical examiners would have to make that determination. "But it is a cruel thing for someone to do such a thing to another human being, is it not?"

I lost it then. He was very kind and his voice was tender, and I could feel my shoulders heave and I couldn't stop. It was the most convulsively I had cried in my life. Just as Burton had done earlier, the captain wrapped his arms around me. I dropped my head on his shoulder and let the tears flow. He spoke in soft, quiet tones. "There, there, my little one." He patted my head gently as he might to comfort a child.

When I calmed a little, he pulled a clean handkerchief from his pocket and handed it to me. I wore no makeup and didn't worry about what my face looked like, but I completely soiled his handkerchief.

I handed it back.

"I have another one if —"

"No," I said. "I'm better now. Thank you."

When I finally turned to leave, he said quietly, "It is none of my business, of course, but I do hope you and Mr. Burton will patch up your — your differences."

"How did you know who — ?"

"What is the word in English? Lovesick, is it? That is how he looks at you. I had

84

noticed it earlier," he said and smiled.

I wanted to tell him that it was impossible for us to patch things up and that Burton and I would never get back together. But I couldn't say those words — in fact, I couldn't trust my voice again. I turned and left the dining room.

12

When I searched for Twila, I had hurriedly raced in and out of her room. Hours later, as I left the dining room, I realized that something about Twila's room hadn't been right. At that time I was more concerned about finding her than anything else. I decided I needed to go back to the room. To my surprise, I felt no trepidation or new wave of sadness. I made my way back to her cabin and opened the door, snapped on the light, and stared. On my previous visit, I hadn't paid attention to anything in the room itself. This time I stared at an opened suitcase. Twila never would have left a suitcase out and opened. She was too neat.

I entered the cabin and closed the door behind me. I don't think anything had changed in the few hours since I had last been there. After I stepped inside, I stood quietly, allowing my eyes to get a sense of the room. Now I saw what it was that had only barely registered in my mind.

The room wasn't torn up — I had seen that kind of situation before — but it wasn't tidy. It was even more than the open suitcase. If I hadn't been so focused on finding Twila the first time, I probably would have noticed.

Her bed wasn't made. I didn't know her habits that well, but it didn't seem consistent with Twila for her not to make the bed. Maids came every third day, so most of us made our own beds. Twila wasn't compulsive, but she was one of those people who lived with the idea of "a place for everything and everything in its place." In fact, she had quoted that to me a couple of times.

Surely Twila never would have left the room for breakfast that morning with a messed-up bed. I wasn't sure, but my immediate hunch was that someone had pulled up the mattress as if searching to see if she had hidden anything under it.

The suitcase was wide open on the desk. Why wouldn't she have laid the suitcase on the bed? It was certainly large enough and a natural spot — only a foot or so from the closet. As I stared at her suitcase, her clothes seemed to be carelessly stuffed back inside. Again, that was not Twila.

The door of the small closet was closed,

but when I opened it, I saw that her clothes, no longer on hangers, had been carelessly dropped or thrown on the floor, and her second suitcase — empty — was on top of the clothes.

At that moment, the obvious truth stuck me: Someone had searched her cabin.

"Why?" I asked aloud.

On one shelf lay her jewelry — a couple of necklaces, three or four sets of earrings, and two bracelets. All of the items were expensive; Twila never bought cheap jewelry.

On the floor, next to the desk, lay her briefcase and her purse. All of us left our purses in our rooms most of the time, so that wasn't unusual. The purse was open, and I saw that the items had been hastily thrown inside — again that wasn't Twila.

The briefcase lay on its side. Some of the papers had been carelessly strewn on the floor. I scanned them quickly, but none of them seemed significant. Aside from a few letters that she probably planned to post on our return to Ushuaia, the rest of the papers were travel folders, instructions about the cruise, and maps — that sort of thing.

Inside the middle section of the briefcase was a selection of books. Automatically I counted them: She had brought six books on the cruise — that was typical of Twila.

Even when we met for lunch, she always carried a book. "In case I have to wait a few minutes," she said. "It helps me not to notice when the other person is late." She seemed always to get to restaurants at least five minutes ahead of her reservation.

I stood next to the desk and stared around the cabin. It was about eight feet wide and perhaps twelve feet long. There wasn't a lot of extra space. It was obvious someone had been inside her cabin and had searched for something.

"I wonder what it was?" I asked aloud.

"I wonder if the person found it?" I answered myself.

"What would Twila have that someone wanted?" Sometimes I talk out loud to myself, especially when I feel confused. I also answer myself, which to most people must sound strange, but that's who I am.

"How could she possibly have anything that would be important enough to kill her for?"

"You're assuming, Julie, that the murder and the search were done by the same person."

"Of course. Don't be stupid!" I said. "Why else would the room look like this?"

"Robbery?"

I shook my head. "No, her wallet is in her

purse with money inside. Her jewelry is still here."

"Okay, then it must have been a search for something significant and —"

"Oh, don't be dense. I know that."

"Okay, smart mouth, what is it?"

I didn't know how to answer myself on that one, so I only shook my head.

Just then the door opened. I looked up and Burton stood in the doorway. He moved inside and closed the door behind him. "Looks as if we both have the same idea. It's not as bad as room 623. Remember that room at —"

"No, it's not." I stopped him. I didn't want to go back to that time. Not only had we worked on a murder case in a hotel, but it was also the time when my life changed. That's when I knew I believed. That's also when Burton realized I loved him. I didn't want to go back to that again.

"Okay, I apologize. I know you don't want to talk about anything personal with me, but —"

"That's right. And you might as well know something else right now." I heard the harshness in my voice. He looked so sad and so much like a boy consumed with grief, I had to harden my emotions to talk to him. I turned away from him and stared at the messy desk.

"Listen, Burton, I came on this cruise only because Twila begged me to."

"I understand, and I don't blame you."

That statement almost broke me. Almost.

"We don't have to have any personal involvement," he said. "I mean between us." He sat on the edge of the bed — which was the only place to sit unless he took the chair that I leaned against.

"Suits me." I'm good at showing suppressed anger. I sat down and folded my arms.

"I have no idea who killed Twila." He leaned forward and stared at the floor. "I have no idea why. If I ever met a true, living saint . . ."

I almost could have written those words for him. When he paused after his long list of Twila's virtues, I said, "Yes, I agree." I hoped he would change his line of thinking. I didn't like playing the hard-hearted soul with the mention of Twila's name. I was trying to decide if I should walk past him or wait until he left.

"This much I know. You didn't kill her, because you were her best friend."

Despite my resolve, I could feel the tears glistening in my eyes. "She told me that," I said.

"She also told me. She gave me quite a lecture after our breakup. She didn't know the reason — and I'm grateful to you for keeping that our secret — but she lectured me for maybe twenty minutes."

"No, please," I said. He was moving back into dangerous emotional waters again. "Don't —"

"You see, I didn't want to come on the cruise because — because I knew it would be uncomfortable for me. And probably just as uncomfortable for you."

"I had the same feeling."

"She insisted," he said.

"With me, as well."

"I mentioned this because I have a point. What I've said and what you said leads to the other thing I know: I didn't kill her. There are forty-six passengers on this ship that knew Twila before we sailed. We can probably eliminate the twenty members of the crew. Agree?"

"Yes." I couldn't look at him. His words were warming my heart, and I didn't want to melt in his presence.

"Why can't we — you and I — investigate this together? It will be two days before we're back to Ushuaia."

I thought of the same thing — probably about the same time he had, but I wasn't ready to say yes.

"On this other thing — this thing about me —"

I could see he fumbled for words. That was something I'd never seen Burton do before. I wasn't going to help him by filling in helpful words.

"You're correct that I have to make things right. I — I don't know how —"

"Sure you do. It's easy. You just tell the truth. Or to put it in your language, you confess your sins."

"But I can't. I'm not thinking about myself. Please believe me. I can't hurt them —"

"I think we've been through this dialogue before. Right?" I was in control of my emotions again. I had to stay in control, or I'd rush over and hug him.

He faced me. He had no tears in his eyes, but it was what I would call the look of the damned. The pain was deeply etched on his face, as if the world was coming to an end, and he had to face God without being ready. I had to look away. I fumbled through the loose papers on the desk.

"I'm working on this — this issue," he said softly. "I want to make things right. Please, please be patient with me."

"It's not a matter of my patience. It's a

matter of your integrity." I love it when I can talk like that. I knew I had hit him hard, and it made me feel just a trifle smug.

"I'll try it again. Just give me a breather on this."

"You make it sound as if I'm *your* pastor." That was a good jab, and I felt a moment of triumph. I had stuck in the knife and twisted it. Sure, I was being mean, but my snide comments were the only way I knew to hold back my emotions.

"Can you — please, can you put our situation on hold until after — ?"

"*Our* situation?" That was the coldest my voice had sounded.

"Julie, please let me say this one thing and hold off your defensive tactics and smart cracks."

I closed my eyes and waited. That's why I love that man. He sees right through me.

"You're totally right. I know that. I've known all along. This is a burden I've carried for a long, long time. You understand the reason I've been quiet all these years, even though what I did was wrong. It was sin. I assure you that I will resolve this. I will make it right."

"Convince me." I didn't want to open my eyes and look at him, but I couldn't help myself.

"I can't. I mean not yet. But I'm convinced God will help me break through on this. The primary reason I finally agreed to come on the cruise was so I could think all this through. I've been tormented, seeking a solution without hurting *them* with the truth that —"

"Don't try to make me part of your problem."

He nodded slowly. "You're right. Forgive me." He reached for my hand. "It's just — it's just that I love you so much, and in the past we've been able to talk so freely —"

"Don't!" I stood up. "Don't . . . talk . . . that . . . way!"

He blushed — he actually blushed in embarrassment. "I apologize. Please accept my apology for doing that."

I turned away. I didn't want to look at his face. "Apology accepted."

"In the meantime, please, can we work on this — this case together?"

When he inserted the word *please,* he got to me. What's worse, he didn't do that deliberately. Manipulating people is not the way Burton thinks. Those words came from his heart. The rat! I hate it when he touches my tender emotions.

He stared at me, waiting for me to respond.

I took a deep breath and nodded.

"I loved her, too, you know," he said. "I wasn't her best friend like you, but she and I had a warm relationship. It was deeper than a pastor-parishioner relationship."

"I know." I have no idea how I hardened my voice on those two words, but I did. I struggled to stay in control of my feelings. I was afraid I wasn't going to win.

"Fine, then," he said. "Let's start with what we know, which isn't much."

"We know she left the ship," I said. "All forty-seven of us left. Zodiac one left with only eleven people. The other three left the ship full — twelve each."

"I was in the first one." He turned his head away as he added, "I wanted to get to Brown Bluff before you so I — so I wouldn't have to see you."

Instead of responding to that statement, I said, "I waited for the third one." I didn't tell him that I had watched the people line up and wanted to put space between us. I watched him get into the first Zodiac. I stood out of the way and went in the third one. "That means she was on the fourth Zodiac. We already know that, but I'm not sure that makes any difference, does it?"

He shook his head. "I don't think so." He held a small sheet of paper. "I wrote down the names of the twelve people on the fourth Zodiac, but I don't think it matters."

He read them aloud: Twila, Donny Otis, Pat Borders, Heather Wilson, Thomas Tomlinson, Mickey Brewer, Sue Downs, Jeff Adams, Betty Freeman, and Shirley and Frank Brackett. "Number twelve, Jon Friesen, went over with them but not back. And that's beyond any question."

"I didn't pay much attention to anyone. The weather had started to turn bad. Jon was in our Zodiac, but I didn't notice he'd switched."

"He said he vomited after the Zodiac started," Burton said, "and someone — I've forgotten who — said that was true."

"Could be," I said. "I had my back to the others. I didn't look at anyone. I was doing a lot of soul-searching —"

"About?"

I wasn't going to open myself up to him on that one. Instead, I said, "I didn't pay attention to anyone; I didn't look at anyone. I was caught up in my own — well, my own thoughts."

"I think we can eliminate Friesen," he said. "He left early."

"Unless — unless he, uh, you know, did the deed first and —"

"Maybe." He paused and thought about

that for a few seconds. "Yes, maybe, but I think we need to focus first on the rest of those in the fourth group."

"Someone — one of the ten people who got into the Zodiac — told Ivan that two people had gone back on the other craft."

"Exactly what I was thinking."

"Ivan didn't say so," I said, "but we all assume the person who said that also got into the Zodiac."

"What if it was someone else?"

"It doesn't make sense to me otherwise. Regardless, we know beyond doubt that Jon Friesen left on the third Zodiac."

"Yes, and your Zodiac — the third one — was already gone before the last one loaded."

I closed my eyes, trying to remember. "I'm not sure. I mean, but I have a vague sense that we left within a minute or two of each other. The weather —"

"That's right," he said. "The last two Zodiacs cut their time short and —"

"I think that's correct." I remembered then. "Yes, that's correct. I had just gotten my boots hosed, and I saw the fourth Zodiac approaching. Not that it makes a lot of difference, does it?"

"Probably not," he said. "But we definitely don't want to forget that there were thirteen people in the third Zodiac — including you — that left perhaps one or two minutes before the last Zodiac."

I didn't reply. That's the problem I have with Burton. We think so much alike. We had gotten so close we could almost finish each other's sentences.

Just then the door opened.

13

"What are you two doing in Twila's cabin?" she asked.

I stared at Heather.

"I think we have the same question for you," Burton said.

"I don't know, exactly," she said. "I thought — oh, I suppose I think I'm Miss Marple, but you know, I thought I might find something —"

"That's why we're here," I said.

"Who could have done such a terrible, terrible thing?" Heather asked.

Neither of us answered. I wanted to learn how distraught she really was. It's not that I didn't believe her story, but she had been one of the ten in the fourth Zodiac, so that put her on the suspect list.

"She was absolutely the sweetest, kindest —"

I stopped listening to the litany. I never would have called Twila *sweet*. She wasn't that kind of person. But there was something about her that drew people to herself. She was also an absolutely no-nonsense person. She rarely used warm, cuddly words like a lot of people. She wasn't much of a hugger, either. Perhaps it was because she was a psychiatrist, but she wouldn't allow people to justify their bad behavior or wrong thinking. She wasn't rude, but she had a way of smiling, looking deeply into a person's eyes, and saying something like, "Is that what you truly believe?"

As far as I know, it always worked. People instinctively trusted her. Twice I had been standing next to her at church and saw her give that look — that's what I called it, the Twila look — and both times the other person stopped lying and opened up to her.

My mind must have wandered, because Heather Wilson was apologizing for trying to play sleuth. As she talked, her eyes darted around the room. I had the impression that she was more interested in seeing if we had discovered anything than she was in finding clues.

"You're sure you didn't notice Twila on Brown Bluff?" Burton asked.

"No, no, I didn't see her — I mean, I didn't recognize her — I mean, well, you know —"

"Yes, we all look quite a bit alike," Burton said.

As I listened to her stumble around, I knew something wasn't right. Either Heather was lying, or she was holding something back. I watched the interchange between them and tried to envision Heather Wilson as someone who carried a knife. She didn't seem to be the kind to stab someone with a literal knife, but I'll bet her words cut deeply.

It was difficult for me to be objective about that woman. I didn't like her; I didn't trust her. I didn't — all right, I was jealous. She's prettier than I am, and men's gazes follow her whenever she walks across the room. I probably secretly wished she were the killer.

With a deep sigh, I pushed aside my negative feelings about Heather.

It seemed obvious that whoever killed Twila had brought the knife — if it was a knife — hidden deeply inside checked luggage. Anything in the hand luggage would have been confiscated.

Of course, there was the possibility that someone had bought a knife at Ushuaia. For two reasons that didn't feel right to me. First, it would be easy enough to check. The business section of Ushuaia wasn't that large. Second, it would mean either that the murderer had left that part of the crime to chance or that the plan to murder Twila hadn't begun until then. I didn't know, of course, but it made sense to assume that the murderer had decided to kill her before we left Atlanta.

Planned it? Planned to kill Twila?

As repugnant as that thought was, I assumed it had been carefully thought out, and the killer waited for the opportunity. Otherwise, it probably would have happened on the first landing.

Another thought that occurred to me was that if it had been a crime of passion, it probably would have occurred aboard ship. I couldn't believe it would have started at Brown Bluff. The cold and the horrible weather didn't allow for a lot of conversation.

Yet another thought struck me: If Twila had had any kind of confrontation or argument with anyone, I'm sure I would have known. She was a professional, but she was also sensitive and easily hurt by harsh or cruel remarks. She wouldn't ever tell me who said them or what they said, but twice in the past she had opened up and talked about mean-spirited words hurled at her. She had said absolutely nothing along that line since we left Atlanta.

That forced me to conclude that someone had planned to kill her before we left Atlanta and had waited for the opportunity to do so.

I stared again at Heather as she talked to Burton. Her eyes never seemed to focus on one spot. She was nervous about the murder, I'm sure, but there was something more.

"Did you have anything in mind when you came here?" I asked her.

"Why, no — I mean, uh, what would I look for?"

"Then how would you know if you found it?"

Heather's laugh had a forced tone to it. "Yes, yes, it does seem a little silly, doesn't it?"

"A little," I said. I tried to give her the Twila look to see if it made a difference.

"I mean, what would I look for?"

"Yes, exactly," I said in my most sarcastic tone. "What *would* you look for?"

"I mean, even if I found it, I wouldn't know what I found, now, would I?"

"I don't know. Would you?" I stayed with the Twila look.

"Uh, well, uh, I suppose I ought to go

back to my cabin," she said, but she didn't move.

She wasn't going to tell me, and I don't think she wanted me to stay around. And that fact had nothing to do with the death of Twila. So I said, "Burton and I have a couple of things to talk about."

"You mean you've found something?"

"Nothing," Burton said.

I tried once more. "Unless you have something specific you want to —"

"No, no —"

"We'll join the others shortly." I turned to Burton. I hoped that showed some kind of dismissal.

She still didn't move.

I stared directly at her, and dim lights seemed to turn on inside her head. I think she assumed that Burton and I were talking romance or reconciliation.

"Oh, oh yes, I understand," she said as if she had just caught on. She gave me what I assume she considered a sincere smile. It was as phony as the color of her dyed hair.

"I'm so glad," I said in a soft voice as sweetly as I knew how.

Heather glared at me, turned, and left the cabin. She didn't close the door, and I wouldn't have put it past her to stand outside and listen.

I closed the door behind her and stood there for a minute with my back against it. I then explained to Burton my thought processes about the killer.

He listened, nodded slowly. "Agreed."

"But to think someone planned —"

"Would it really matter whether it was out of sudden, uncontrollable anger or planned out of long-held anger?"

"I suppose not."

I hadn't heard any noise in the hallway, so I assumed Heather had gone. I walked over to the desk and sat on the chair. My gaze slowly swept every part of the room. I stared momentarily at the mattress. I got up to look under it, but Burton beat me to it. He lifted the mattress and found nothing.

"Let's think about this," I said. "Twila obviously had something the murderer wanted."

"Agreed."

"That person may have searched this room after killing her."

Burton pondered that one. "Agreed."

"We can also assume that whatever *it* is must be incriminating enough or important enough for someone to kill her to get it."

"Agreed."

"But Twila?" I asked. "I thought everyone trusted her. Even if she knew something —"

"As a professional —"

"She wouldn't tell."

"But what if —," Burton said and paused before adding, "the murderer either didn't know that or was afraid that Twila *would* tell."

"Agreed," I said and tried to emulate his voice.

He gave me a faint smile. "I love it when you mock me."

I chose to ignore that. "Then it would have to be something illegal. We're therapists, but the law doesn't require us to report confessions —"

"But you know Twila. If someone confessed a crime to her — especially a serious crime — she would have pushed that person to confess."

"Agreed," I said. This time I don't think he heard me.

He paced the small room several times, and all the while he seemed to scrutinize each section of the cabin.

"She once told me that one of her clients had embezzled almost a million dollars," I said, "and he confessed because he couldn't live with his crime."

"Did she report it?"

"Better than that: She convinced him to confess."

"That sounds like Twila."

"Oh, but here's the good part. His corporation — a large one, I understand — rehired him. They put him in security. He had been so good at what he did, no one ever discovered it."

"So I suppose his new job was to catch others —"

"That's what Twila told me," I said.

He smiled at me, and I looked away. When he does that, I can hardly resist him. He has those movie-star teeth and a smile that's so genuine I had to do something to keep my resolve.

"So where do we go from here?" I asked.

"I don't know," Burton said, "but I thought that by putting our minds together, we might come up with something."

This time I shut up and waited for him to speak. I knew he was thinking about the two murder cases we had worked on together. I'm sure he also knew that's what I was thinking about.

"Do you remember when — ?" he asked.

"Yes, but let's focus on now."

"Agreed." This time he imitated me imitating him.

I tried to maintain a serious expression, but that made me laugh even more. I held up my hand. "Okay, let's focus."

For the next half hour we threw out ideas but came up with nothing concrete. Both of us knew all the passengers in the fourth Zodiac. To us, the ten people still seemed the most likely suspects.

"Unless —," I said.

"Unless what?"

"Unless the person who said two people were going in the other Zodiac was not only the killer but a passenger in the other boat."

"Do you mean Jon Friesen?"

"Not necessarily. That would mean it was the killer who brought the message."

"It doesn't register with me," Burton said, "but I don't want to disregard that possibility."

"The messenger had to be the killer."

"Agreed."

"The question is whether the killer was one of the ten people who went back or —"

"Yes, true," Burton said. "But let's focus on this. We can assume that whoever told Ivan about two passengers not being on his Zodiac was the killer."

"Elementary, my dear Watson," I said.

He laughed. "That's better than *agreed.*"

I thought so, too, but I was creeping near the edge again, so I said, "But if we assume the killer got into Ivan's Zodiac, that means we've narrowed the suspect list. Ivan said he thought it was a man who told him that two of them went in the other boat."

"But he also said he wasn't sure. He had been distracted —"

"By the reprimand on the radio," I finished. "Makes sense."

Burton went to the closet. He took out the suitcase and ran his hands across the lining. He found nothing. He picked up each item of clothing, one at a time. He said nothing, but I watched him. He's a neatnik, too, and he carefully folded each item and laid it carefully inside the suitcase. Frankly, Burton is more detail oriented than I am, so I knew he'd do a better job of searching.

He began to examine the three small shelves where she stored her underwear and jewelry.

I laughed. "Let me look there," I said. "I think that's more of a woman's task."

He moved out of the way, and I carefully looked at each item of jewelry without touching. They seemed to be neatly stored as if no one had disturbed them. It was the same with the underwear. The person who had been careless in the other part of the room hadn't disturbed anything.

"I'm going to assume that it was something fairly large," I said.

"Agreed — uh, elementary, Dr. Watson."

He winked at me, but I turned away so he couldn't see the smile on my face.

"What do you think it was? A letter? A file folder? A book?" Burton said.

"Probably, but why would anyone want to steal something like a file unless it contained something incriminating? Maybe it was a large envelope with —" I stopped. "Wait! A book! Maybe it was a book. Look in her briefcase. She carried six books with her. I counted them."

He pulled them out. All but one of them had dust jackets. The one without a dust jacket was *Gifted Hands.* He read the other titles: "We have *When Someone You Love Abuses Alcohol or Drugs, 90 Minutes in Heaven, Think Big, Heaven Is Real,* and *Gifted Hands.*"

Again, both of us had the same thought. He snatched the *Gifted Hands* dust jacket off the last book. The title revealed definitely wasn't *Gifted Hands.*

I stood next to Burton as he opened it. It was some kind of self-published book titled *Wasted Life.* Twila's name was at the bottom.

Both of us skimmed the first few pages, and I shook my head. "It has Twila's name, but that's not Twila's voice."

14

"Just read it yourself," I said. "That doesn't sound like Twila."

"I thought the same thing. This sounds more — more academic —"

"More like case studies," I said. "We had tons of them during our student days."

"Case studies," he said again.

We stared at each other.

"Case studies," I echoed.

"Of course! That's what it is!" he answered.

I took the book out of his hands. "Look, it's not really bound like a regular book. It only looks that way."

"You're right." He pointed to a page where Twila had red-lined a sentence and added a full paragraph in the margin in her small, back-slanted style.

"You know what I think?" I said. "I think —"

"She had started to teach a course this

semester at Clayton University." He smiled at me as if he had just figured it out. "I'll bet these are her lectures."

I started to say, "Agreed," but decided we'd worn out that joke. "That's exactly what I started to say." In spite of myself, I smiled when I spoke those words. It felt good — and familiar — to banter again with Burton.

"And this had to be important enough for her to put on a false dust jacket to disguise it," he said.

"Let's assume she did that on purpose."

"Could it have been otherwise?"

I thought about the question and tried to make a case inside my head for a mistake on her part. "You're right."

"So if she did it intentionally," he said, "she —"

"She was suspicious."

"Probably," he said.

That made sense to me. "But why?"

We skimmed the first fifty pages of the book. She had obviously written the manuscript with a scholarly approach, as we had already noted. She was careful not to use names but only initials. Because I knew Twila, I had a strong feeling that even the initials weren't the true ones.

"Where's the key?" Burton asked. "There

must be some way to figure out who these people are."

She had twenty-one case studies. The premise of the book was that each of them had been headed toward a wasted life. The causes varied, but each of them had come to see her professionally and had become her clients.

Burton stood behind me to read over my shoulder.

I read through the introduction and went back to something I had skimmed. Her point was that too many people waste their lives instead of getting help — and not just any kind of help. She felt they needed to find the type of treatment that worked for them.

As a therapist, I was familiar with each method. Cognitive behavioral therapy worked for some, psychoanalysis for others. She talked about the value of Gestalt and RET or rational-emotive therapy. Burton had a vague idea about them, but I explained how Twila had distinguished between Freudian and Jungian analysis. I added, "Twila personally advocated psychodynamic therapy."

"What's that?" he asked.

I had hoped he'd give me a chance to say something to show off a little of my training. "Psychodynamic therapy is more long term and deals with deep-seated patterns *formed in childhood.*" I emphasized those three words, but he didn't react.

Burton skimmed the rest of the potential procedures and chuckled. "And some benefit from deep-body massage?"

"Oh yes, it has helped some."

"That's a new one to me."

"It's still around because it works for some people," I said. "It's not what I use or anything I see practiced much in Clayton County, but that doesn't make it useless."

"What is it, exactly?" he asked.

Again, I hoped I would get a response — any kind of response from him. I pointed to a paragraph where she insisted that deep-body massage had produced results for some practitioners. She also stated that it must be used only by someone who understands the body. I pointed to her reference to biogenetic analysis.

He didn't react, so I added, "Biogenetic analysis is a kind of mind-body connection. I don't hear much about it today. The expression most often used — thirty years ago — was having someone beat the ground with a stick or some angry repetitive action —"

"Why?"

"To bring emotions to the fore. The idea was that we store memories in various places in our body, especially bad memories."

I saw a flicker — quick, furtive — but I had gotten a reaction. He dropped his head and read some more.

I had tried, and I knew that was the only response I was going to get from him. He always says that Christians try to take over God's work and become the conscience for others. *I might as well surrender this to the Lord,* I thought. *I'm not making any progress with him.*

I turned back to what Twila had written. She made references to medication and stated that many of the popular drugs only masked symptoms so that clients didn't have access to their pain. She wasn't against such drugs but advocated stringent, careful prescription.

Twila devoted four pages to faith. She stated that she'd had considerable success with those who came to her about their desire for faith in their lives. She said that she wrote this with "positive prejudice toward the topic" and made a case for the transforming power of the Christian faith, "which I have followed since I was fourteen years old."

I was familiar with the various theories, of course, but I had never run across a psychiatrist who actually advocated the "different strokes for different folks" idea. Of the twenty-one case histories, before they became her patients, all of them had previously been to psychiatrists, psychics, analysts, faith healers, and counselors of every type, even exorcists.

Twila made an important note that she had changed a few details about the individuals to protect their identities. "I can say with absolute certainly that fourteen of these clients are quite healthy and no longer need any psychiatric help. Four of the cases, despite five to twelve years of care, are still symptomatic. Three of them are functional but are characterologically impaired."

"What does 'characterologically impaired' mean?" Burton asked.

"They would fall into the category of personality disorders." I enjoy playing knowledgeable occasionally. "While they appear normal in everyday social situations, they have persistent traits that aren't obvious on the surface."

"I'm not clear —"

"Try this," I said. "People with personality disorders don't think they have any problems, but those who know such people have problems with them."

"Such as?" Burton asked.

Immediately I thought of an example. "Paranoid personalities might secretly believe everyone is out to get them. If you didn't know about that secret belief, their behaviors might not make sense."

He got it, so we continued to look at her manuscript. For each case, she went through a three-to-five-page history about their condition, how long they had been aware of their symptoms, and what treatment they had received.

She wrote another section of about the same length in which she described her diagnosis (which was occasionally quite different from previous diagnoses), what she had done, and how long she had worked with the client. She also included her discharge notes. For Twila, discharge included dropping out of treatment, being referred to another therapist because she didn't feel they had made significant progress with her, or mutually agreeing to terminate therapy.

What surprised me was her assertion that in many instances, professional interventions were no more effective than intervention by a friend, a pastor, or someone who could *listen uncritically* and *accept the other person without restriction or condition.* "Such caring individuals seem to be in great demand but short supply. Hence, the needy individuals feel they have to resort to professional help." She listed one caveat — unless there was evidence of psychosis. In that case, she would treat the person with medication.

Although she occasionally had a snappy, well-worded sentence, her writing was what I'd call turgid. If she could find a simple word, she didn't use it but threw in a lot of psychiatric jargon and never settled for five words when she could write twenty. Because her audience was primarily grad students, that made sense to me.

Burton and I stared at the book. He took it from me and leafed through the entire manuscript, which ran about 250 pages, single-spaced, in ten-point type.

"What do you think?" he asked.

"My assumption is that whoever killed her is one of those three incorrigibles," I said.

"That's logical, but —"

"I know. We can't prove it. In fact, we can't prove anything —"

"But it's as good a place to start as any," he said.

I wanted to say to him, "Please stop finishing my sentences." I didn't. He had been accurate each time. But I had to remind myself that I wasn't supposed to like him very much right now. Yet how could I remain aloof with a person like Burton who thinks the same way I do?

"We don't know the identity of any of them, especially the three that —"

"That's exactly what I started to say," I said.

He shrugged and gave me that gorgeous, heart-melting smile. "Maybe that's why we work so well together."

I chose to ignore that. "Do you suppose she left some kind of key?" I asked instead of answering him. "Surely she had some way to track and keep twenty-one identities separate."

"Of course she did," Burton said. "I assume it'll be somewhere in her office —"

"Which we don't have access to right now!" In spite of myself, I giggled. I had finished *his* sentence.

"That's what I was going to say."

"Oh, really?" I tried to act surprised. "You know, I read somewhere that if two people think the same way, one of them isn't necessary."

"Ah, but they don't know us. They obviously didn't know people who could —"

"Right, but let's focus on this situation."

I closed my eyes and thought about Twila's habits. She had a phenomenal memory. So it was possible she hadn't needed any written key.

I mentioned that to Burton, and he said, "And if she was concerned enough to use a false cover —"

"We can assume that the murderer could very well be one of the people named in her book — her lectures." I thought for a moment. "Something else," I said. "The killer must have known about the book or that she had something in writing —"

"Or he wouldn't have searched."

"Or she," I added.

"I stand corrected. It could be a woman. Anyone can plunge a knife into someone."

"Or whatever it was." Again I mentioned that someone would have had to bring the weapon inside checked luggage. I was thinking out loud. As Burton had long known, I sometimes do my best thinking when I talk.

"I don't know where anyone could have picked up a knife in Buenos Aires, because we never left the airport. In Ushuaia it doesn't seem likely, either. How many stores did you see?"

"Aside from restaurants, I'd say not more than a dozen."

"Too easy to trace and —"

"How would the person know that she or he would be able to buy a knife in Ushuaia?"

"Unless that person had an accomplice on the ship." Even as I said the words, I knew that idea seemed too far-fetched.

"Conspiracy theory?" Burton said. "Nah, I don't think so."

"I don't, either."

"I know," he said. "And I doubt that we'll find the knife or whatever it was. There is a big ocean on all sides of this ship. Too easy to get rid of."

"Agreed," I said. This time I tried hard to imitate his way of talking and cocked my head slightly, just the way he did.

He laughed. "You do me quite well."

"Yes, I know."

"You're playful and cute when you do it, too."

I think I blushed, but I had to admit to myself that I had never known anyone in my life who understood me — and especially my humor — like Burton.

"I've missed your smart mouth," he said softly. "I've missed it a lot."

"I missed someone to practice on," I said and immediately regretted it. I held up my hand. "Okay, that's the end of that road. Let's detour. I don't want to fall into our old way of talking and interacting."

He only nodded. A few seconds later, he asked, "What if we let it slip that we had found — ?"

"The book?" I said. "Yes —"

"Agreed." I saw the merriment in his eyes, but I didn't give way to my feelings. Instead, I took the book from him, pulled out the first half of the pages, and gave him the rest. He had the *Gifted Hands* dust cover, and I took it from him to keep my pages together. I made a loose fold and put it inside the large pocket of my heavy jacket.

I didn't understand much, but I sensed that Twila's book of lectures would lead us to the killer.

15

Burton and I talked for several minutes longer in Twila's cabin. No matter where we took our thinking, it always came back to her lecture book.

Hours later and unable to think of anything new, we went to see Captain Robert. He was in the lounge, setting up a film about plant life on Antarctica. I had already read about the subject in the *Explore Antarctica* guidebook. The fact that earlier explorers found lichen meant they could classify Antarctica as a continent. By contrast, nothing grew on or around the Arctic ice cap, so it wasn't a continent.

The captain said he was finished with his work and motioned for us to sit down. Without asking, he brought each of us a bottle of cold Coca Cola and a glass.

"You already know quite a bit about us, I assume," Burton said.

"Not really so much," he said.

In a space of twenty minutes, we told him the story of how we had been thrown together eighteen months earlier at Palm Island, off the coast of Georgia. We arrived at the island after the death of the host, Roger Harden. Because the others were already on the island when the murder was committed, and the police couldn't get to the island until the next day, we had worked together and solved the crime.

Ten months later we ran into each other at the Cartledge Inn near Stone Mountain, Georgia. Again there was a murder, and we worked together to solve that one.

"So now you are here and you will solve this murder, is that not so?" Captain Robert asked. At first I thought he was being cynical, but as I looked at his face, I knew he had asked a serious question.

"We would like to try," Burton said.

"As I told you earlier . . ." Once again without warning, my eyes clouded with tears. "Twila Belk was my best friend."

"I was her pastor," Burton said. "She was also like a second mother. I have to do what I can."

"Of course, you must do what you can," the captain said. "I cannot give you official permission to do this, but I shall assist you in any way possible."

"Will you encourage the others to co-operate with us?" I asked.

The captain pondered the question for a few minutes before he answered. "Yes, yes, I can do that." He also said he would come to the dining room during breakfast, which was served at seven, and speak to the passengers.

We thanked the captain and left him.

I was tired but didn't know if I could sleep. I went into the room and didn't bother to undress. I was sure I would lie awake.

The next moment of awareness was when I looked at my watch. It was 5:30 a.m. Despite the rocking of the waves, I had slept an hour or two.

I wanted to stay in the room and read, but I didn't dare. Betty was likely to awaken. She's one of those people who loves to talk when she has nothing to say. Harmless enough, I suppose, but it was tiring to listen to her constant chatter. I'd tried several times to turn her off by mumbling an occasional word or nodding while my mind focused on other things. She had the most disconcerting habit of punctuating every second sentence with my name. Hearing my name snapped me back to attention, and I resented it. I enjoyed my own thoughts more.

I hurried to the bathroom for a one-handed shower. After I dressed, I put the pages I'd torn from Twila's manuscript in my shoulder bag and went to the dining room. A small light glowed so no one would knock over the furniture. I snapped on a lamp in the far corner and sat down. I laid my shoulder bag on the table, pulled out Twila's case studies, and began to read. Although I had no idea of the identity of any of the clients, the studies fascinated me. Despite the formal tone, Twila had been meticulous in her details. She clearly delineated between the objective results of tests and her own interpretations.

I must have dozed off, because I awakened to the aroma of freshly brewed coffee. I got up and poured myself a cup. As I drank, I looked around. Burton was asleep in the corner. He had probably been there the entire time.

I must have awakened him, because he looked up and stretched. "Is the coffee good?"

"Is that the masculine way of asking me to bring you a cup?"

"You catch on quickly," he said and stretched again.

I poured him a cup, added a spoon of milk, and carried it to him. As I walked toward him, I was ready to make another smart-mouthed remark, but the cad beat me to it.

"Keep it up and you'll make a macho type out of me yet and allow you to bring me coffee regularly."

"You make it; I'll pour it," I said and wished I hadn't. Once again, the language was getting too familiar.

Burton thanked me for the coffee and sipped it absently. "I've read about half of my pages. The style doesn't make for great reading —"

"Unless you like to read case studies," I said. "I read hundreds of them during my student days." I took a few sips of my coffee and added, "And I liked them, then. The style hasn't changed, but the material is fascinating."

"If you say so," he said. He went back to his reading.

Both of us focused on the manuscript. Without saying it, I think we realized that time was running out. Our ship would soon navigate the Drake Passage, and many of the passengers would stay in their rooms because of motion sickness.

He stretched and said, "I think it's time

for me to clean up and shave before the others start lining up for the showers." He put his manuscript inside the book cover, took his dirty cup back to the serving table, and left.

I watched him walk away.

Instead of getting further away from the man, I'm getting closer again. That's not what I planned.

16

I had long been impressed with Twila's insight and her amazing intuition about people. But the book amazed me even more. Just from reading the first four case studies, I felt I knew the clients and understood why Twila was such an effective psychiatrist.

"Excuse me," a man's voice said.

I must have jumped. I had been so absorbed in my reading that I hadn't noticed Jon Friesen enter the room. "Sorry, but you startled me."

"May I join you?" he asked. He directed the question to me, but he wasn't looking at my face. Although he was still about eight paces away, his gaze didn't leave the pages. Instinctively I covered them with my hand.

"Or would you prefer — ?"

"No, no, that's fine," I said. "In fact, why don't we have a cup of coffee together?" I wanted to get his attention away from the manuscript. I stood up, turned over the pages, and laid my shoulder bag on top of them.

"Please, allow me to get it for you," he said.

"Thanks. No sugar, no milk. Just coffee."

While he was gone, I put the pages into my shoulder bag. For now, no one except Captain Robert knew that Burton and I had found the manuscript. I wanted to keep that information secret just a little longer.

After Jon handed me the cup, he sat across from me. He had chosen hot chocolate. He sipped the steaming beverage before he said, "That must have been absorbing reading."

I shrugged as if to minimize it.

"But you seemed so engrossed and focused on —"

"I get that way sometimes."

"I assume it's only when something commands your attention."

"Yes, that's true," I said. This conversation was headed in the wrong direction, so I decided to take charge. "Were you looking for me? Or did you just happen to come by and see me here?"

"No, I was looking for you."

"Oh, that makes me feel important. Why were you looking for me?"

"I want to tell you that I'm sorry about the death of Twila. I knew you and she were

131

good friends." He was a tall man, thin and muscular. His face, set in strong lines, was impassive as he spoke. He wore expensive royal blue warm-up pants and a tight off-white polo shirt that made those muscular arms look even more prominent.

"We were more than close friends." I felt my voice begin to falter. Most of the time I was able to push aside my personal sense of loss, but in unexpected moments like this, the feelings overwhelmed me. I turned my face away from him and blinked several times. "I considered her my very, very special friend."

"I am sorry," he said. He reached across the table and laid his hand on mine. "This must be a painful time for you."

"Yes, it is."

"Do you want to talk about it?"

"That's what I usually say to people who hurt."

"Then perhaps we can reverse positions for now," he said. He drew back his hand and got up, came around to my side of the table, and put his arm around my shoulder.

"Please don't," I said. I pulled a tissue out of my bag and wiped my eyes.

Jon sat down and stared at me. He said nothing, as if he expected me to continue.

He won that one. A wave of grief overwhelmed me, and to avoid giving in to my tears, I began to talk. "She introduced herself to me the first time I visited the church." I closed my eyes, and memories filled my mind. The pain was deep, much deeper than I had thought. I shook my head as if the gesture would shake away my grief. "We also became friends that day."

Jon still said nothing, so I talked about the growing relationship between Twila and me. Occasionally Jon made a comment — usually a very professional one, such as "Ah, I see," or "How did you feel?"

After a few minutes, I stopped talking and stared at him. "Are you — or have you ever been — a professional therapist?"

He shook his head. "No, but I've been to a few."

"Want to talk about it?"

"No, I don't think so."

His answer shocked me. First, he didn't laugh or even smile at my quick retort. Almost anyone else would have caught the humor. Burton would have gotten it and given me a clever response. Oh, sometimes he ignored me, but I could always tell he got my meaning. I couldn't read anything from Jon's response.

"Now it's your turn," I said. "You talk and I listen, nod, or say things like 'Go on,' or

'Hmm.' "

"I don't have anything to say."

"You said you've been to a number of therapists."

"Yes, I did. Yes, I have."

I have had a few clients like Jon, and it often takes half an hour or longer to get them to start to talk. Once I get them to open up, they usually sense they can trust me. After that I sometimes have to interrupt them to get them to stop.

I didn't know Jon well. I think we met when he sat next to me in a Sunday school class. He had spoken at most five sentences to me in the months since we'd known each other. I decided to try again. Giving him my best smile and keeping my voice low and soft, I asked, "Did you know Twila well?"

He shook his head. "Not well."

"Then why did she invite you as her guest?"

"She was my therapist for a time."

"For how long a time?"

"Not too long."

"But she was no longer your therapist when you came on the cruise?"

"Correct."

To give myself time to think of a fresh approach, I took a few sips of my now-warm coffee. I studied Jon. It seemed to me that almost everyone at church knew him, and the younger girls referred to him as a hunk or a hottie. He was a couple of inches above six feet, which I liked. His almost-blond hair had a circular part, and his almond-colored eyes showed intensity. He had an incredible bod, and his pecs bulged and rippled when he made the slightest move.

The first time I saw him at church, I envisioned him behaving like a fourteen-year-old and expected him to flex his muscles and ask me to feel his arm. I had done that a few times — when I was thirteen.

"How long is *not long?*"

"A few months."

"How many months is a few? Two? Twelve?" That smart remark would have gotten a good response from Burton.

Jon stared at me. He didn't smile then, and I realized that I had only seen him smile once or twice before.

"You said not long. How long was that?" I persisted.

"Months. Less than a year. I don't remember."

"So you weren't close? I mean, she wasn't what you'd call a friend?"

"No."

"You weren't her friend?" I'm sure the

135

shock showed on my face. "Then what are you doing on this trip?"

17

"I am on this trip to see Antarctica," Jon said. "Isn't that the reason all of us came?"

"But you came as a guest of Twila's."

"Correct."

"You weren't a current client and you weren't a friend?"

"True."

"That surprises me. I mean, she invited only friends and clients on this cruise. Or at least that's what I thought —"

"Perhaps she liked me."

"Perhaps." I decided to play his little game.

Silence filled the room except for faint noises coming from the galley area. A few pots clinked, and someone turned on a spigot. I was going to wait him out.

"I would like to talk to you," Jon said. He paused, lifted his hot chocolate to his mouth to finish it. But he did that muscle flexing at the same time. I suppose most women liked it.

Yes, I liked it, too. He was really quite strikingly handsome.

"I've wanted to talk to you," he said. "I've wanted to talk to you since I first saw you at church."

"Really?"

"Yes."

"But you never said anything."

"True."

This wasn't getting anywhere, so I decided to try a few more words. "So why didn't you talk to me?"

"It was obvious that your attention was focused elsewhere."

"That obvious, was it?"

"To me it was." He tried to sip his hot chocolate again but realized it was gone. He put down his cup and pushed away from the table. "The past few weeks I — I haven't seen you around much."

"You looked for me?"

Those almond-colored eyes seemed intensely focused on me. "Every Sunday."

"Oh."

"So why haven't I seen you?"

"I wasn't around much." I love those smart-mouthed answers, and they irritate Burton. Or at least he tries to make me think they do.

"Yes, I'm aware," he said. "That's why I mentioned it."

I stared at him for several seconds, and he stared back without blinking. I couldn't figure out this man. I tried to remember what I knew about him, which wasn't much. He was a day trader, and the gossip was that he had scored really big just before the dot-com bubble burst. I decided to try the question-and-answer technique.

"You're quite a handsome man. The word I heard is that you're enormously wealthy."

"Yes."

"I also know you're single," I said, "and very attractive to the unattached women at church."

He shrugged as if to say it was of no importance.

This man wasn't going to give out information easily, not even when I flattered him. "Have you ever been married?"

"Yes."

"Yes? What does that mean?"

"That I have not always been single."

In spite of myself, I laughed. His expression didn't change. *What kind of man is this? The outdoor lights shine brightly, but I'm not sure there's anyone alive inside the building.*

"How many times have you not been

single?" If he has any sense of humor, that one ought to get a response.

"Three times."

"Oh, so I suppose you're one of those men who will keep trying until you get it right."

"I will get it right this time if you will marry me."

"Whoa! That's a bit fast," I said. He continued to puzzle me. He was supposed to smile — or at least make an attempt at a smile.

"I like you," he said in a soft, low voice. "Do you like me?"

"I'm not sure about a lot of my feelings right now."

"I'll wait." He stared at me as if he thought he could see inside my head.

"Enough along that line, okay? I don't want to get into anything romantic. Okay? My heart is heavy over the loss of my close friend." *Doesn't the man ever blink?*

"Yes, it is sad."

When we finally were able to talk further — beyond a few syllables at a time — he said the right words. Maybe he was too correct. He reminded me of a few college classmates. We had studied the work of Carl Rogers, who founded the client-centered therapy movement. We learned clever responses such as "I hear you saying . . . ," and we learned to feed people back what they told us in slightly different words. That showed we focused on them. We also learned to use one-word responses — much as Jon had done with me.

The problem with most of those classmates is that they did this by rote. It was if they had been programmed to give the orthodox response. Most of them outgrew their allegiance to pat answers, but Jon sounded as if he were still in Psych 101 or at most 201.

"Have you ever studied Carl Rogers?" I asked.

"No."

"Really?"

"Yes."

"Where did you learn all those phrases you used on me?"

"I have been in therapy."

"Many times?"

"Yes."

"Were you seeing Twila up until the time of the cruise?"

"Do you mean as a patient?"

"Yes."

"No."

"Because — ?"

"Because I was no longer seeing her."

"Oh." Just then I remembered something

Twila had said to me when she first began to plan the cruise. "I want to invite the people I most love from the church," she said. "I'll also invite a few others — people who need me."

I'm not sure if I responded to that statement, although at the time it struck me as odd. But then, I was so fixated on James Burton, I wasn't much interested in the rest of the people.

"That reminds me: You became sick on Brown Bluff."

"No, I got sick before I went to the island."

"Minor point. You were sick, right?"

"Correct. I had slept badly, my stomach was upset, and I was nauseated before I left. I almost vomited on the island, but I began to breathe very slowly because I didn't want to barf on that pristine land. I told someone — and before you ask, I don't know who it was — to tell Ivan that I was sick and would return on the third Zodiac. The people were climbing into it then to return."

That was the most he had spoken at one time. This came across as even stranger than his silence. The words sounded as if he had memorized a page of movie dialogue, and he spoke them like a third-rate actor.

I thought again of the way he talked. I decided his words sounded as if he had memorized a script but had forgotten to add emotions.

He didn't frighten me, but I was confused by his presence. Was he one of the people who needed Twila? When I first began to work for Clayton County Special Services, I met a few people like him. They came across as emotional zombies. Sometimes it was the medication, such as powerful tranquilizers. Sometimes they just had a few unconnected wires inside their heads. None of them had ever been dangerous — as far as I knew — but they're not the kind of people I'd like to invite for dinner.

"Are you on any medication?"

"Sometimes," he said.

"I'm sorry, but I don't understand."

"Sometimes I take it; sometimes I don't."

"Oh."

He said nothing but kept his gaze fixed on me. *Doesn't he ever blink? Don't his eyes dry out staring like that?* I decided to play the stare game.

He won; I blinked and turned away.

I picked up my shoulder bag and got up. He pushed away his chair and stood up next to me. He held out his arms to embrace me, and he did it in such a way as if he expected me to fall into them. That gesture felt strange to me.

143

Instead I took both his hands briefly. "Thank you for opening yourself so fully to me."

"It's because I like you."

"That sounds like my kind of smart-mouth speaking," I said. He didn't get it, so I added, "Thank you." I had no idea why I was thanking him, but I thought, *You figure it out, big dude.*

I walked away from him and headed back to my room. I didn't turn around, but I listened carefully. He hadn't followed me, and I relaxed.

Everything about Jon confused me. No, that's not quite accurate. I had already done a quickie professional analysis — that's one of the hazards of my occupation — and I admitted to myself that it's dangerous to make immediate judgments. But in my thinking, he fit the profile of a man with unstable personal relationships, a self-image that is not well formed, and poor impulse control. His amorous attempts were totally out of context. He had no awareness of me or of my reaction. For lack of a better label, I'd have called him a borderline personality.

He's a little creepy, I thought. *He's a handsome man, but good looks are no insurance against being creepy.* I decided to see if I could look at Twila's file on him when we returned to Georgia.

If he's so strange, Twila certainly knew it. She would have picked that up in about ten seconds. So why did Twila invite him? He must be one of those who needed her. Is he someone capable of killing her? I had no idea.

But for now, there were forty-six passengers on the ship. By eliminating Burton and me, we had forty-four possible-but-remote suspects. If we stayed with the ten who were in the fourth Zodiac, that cut down the task of finding the killer considerably. But Jon had gone to the island on the fourth Zodiac, so I decided to make him number eleven.

"He's slightly nuts," I said aloud. "He's probably not dangerous, but he's still nuts."

"Julie, no professional talks that way," I said to myself.

"Okay, he's at least a borderline personality —"

"Julie!"

"Okay, without further tests, I'd classify him as a person with a borderline personality disorder. We call that BPD."

"Now you sound professional," I said.

"I'd probably also sound crazy if anyone else heard me."

I walked along the outside deck. It was

getting colder, and I pulled my heavy jacket tighter.

"He may be BPD, but that doesn't make him a killer."

18

I went back to the room and found Betty Freeman awake and in her usual chattering mood. She was nearly dressed but couldn't make up her mind whether to wear slacks or her running suit. She started to talk and I gave her only one-word answers, but that didn't stop her.

Finally I gave her nothing but nods. Still she persisted.

"Julie, I heard that you and Burton have received permission to act like detectives and solve this terrible — terrible thing."

That opened me up. "Who said so?"

"I don't know. Gossip among the passengers. Maybe somebody overheard —"

"Or maybe someone was eavesdropping."

She blushed. "Well, I wasn't really, Julie. I mean, I didn't intend to eavesdrop. I was only —"

"It doesn't matter," I said. I wanted her to shut up so I could have peace and quiet.

For thirty seconds, she said nothing. I stretched out on my back on my bunk and closed my eyes.

"Julie, I suppose you'd like to take a nap or something."

"Yes."

"I don't want to disturb you, Julie. I tried to read but couldn't keep my mind on it, don't you know? I get bored walking around on the deck."

I didn't reply.

"I have a question. Please, Julie, don't take offense if I ask, okay?"

"So ask." I sighed loudly, but I knew she wouldn't get the message.

"Burton. Is it over between you two? You know, romantically over?"

"Why do you ask?" That's always a safe question to find out the question behind the question.

"Uh, well, Julie, I — I'm just, uh, you know, I'm a little curious."

"And available."

"Well, yes. And he is so cute, isn't he?" Betty was about half a foot shorter than me. She was about my age, maybe a year or two older. I'm thin and willowy with almost no fat — okay, I'll translate that. I'm not rounded in the right places. Most women complain about their rear ends being too large. I'm so flat everywhere I can wear boys' clothes.

"I mean, dear Julie, if I — if I —"

"He's unattached as far as I'm concerned," I said. I hope I said it with more conviction than I felt. I also wished she'd stop using my name with almost every sentence, so I could tune her out.

She talked on and on. I think it was something about the man she almost married when she was in college. Or maybe it was one of her music professors. I didn't care, and I didn't want to hear.

Most of all, I didn't want to talk about Burton. I wanted to grieve over Twila — and I wanted to think. I finally figured out the only way to do that was to feign sleep. I turned over on my stomach and lay still.

A few minutes later, Betty said, "Well, Julie, you're sure you don't mind?"

I did mind, but I didn't answer. If she could entice him, that was fine. No, it wasn't fine, and I admitted I loved him.

"Aren't you going to breakfast?" I asked to change the subject.

"Sometimes a girl has to watch her figure," she said. "Do you think I've gotten too big in the hips? Maybe I should lose ten pounds. What do you think?"

It was much simpler to pretend to be asleep.

After that she painted her fingernails and toenails. I think I heard her brushing her hair about five hundred times. But I soon pushed her out of my mind.

I missed Twila. I didn't know how I'd function without her friendship. Even though we'd become close only within the last year, it felt as if we'd always known each other.

To distract my own grief, I thought about the book of lectures she had written. I hadn't finished reading my portion of the chapters before Jon interrupted me. I wanted to read more, but if I made the slightest move, Betty would start talking to me again. I thought of going to the lounge, but I assumed other people would be there at this time. Except for mealtime, the others could be almost anyplace on the ship.

My mind stayed on the book. That had to be the answer. Her death. The room searched. The wrong cover on the book — and because I knew Twila, I knew she had not done that mindlessly.

The killer had to be one of the people mentioned in the book. The more I played with that idea, the more sense it made. But she carefully altered the identities, so I don't see how anyone could know he or she was one of the people written about in the book. Twila would never, never knowingly hurt anyone.

As I lay in the almost-quiet room, I vaguely recalled weeks earlier when Twila talked to me about her lectures at Clayton University. She told me that she had disguised the case studies enough so that the individuals wouldn't recognize themselves. She didn't tell me she had written them in a book form.

She told me something else about the case studies. I couldn't quite remember. . . . *What was it?*

I hadn't paid much attention, because it didn't seem important then. I kept trying to replay that moment inside my head. I was actually surprised that I remembered any of it. As I lay on the bunk, I noticed the waves outside weren't yet rough. The gentleness must have rocked me to sleep.

When I awakened, I rolled over onto my back. Betty was gone. She probably decided breakfast was more important than losing ten pounds. I lay quietly for perhaps a minute, allowing my mind to go where it chose.

"What about the legal issues?" I didn't hear a voice, but the words were so loud, I sat up abruptly.

"Yes! Yes, that's what I was trying to remember," I shouted. Twila had said she'd changed enough minor facts that she could disguise the subject without distorting the truth of the case. She had assured me of this when I reminded her of a case I had read about in California. A psychologist did some weird therapy like making everyone scream like a bird or an animal. A writer who documented his practice changed names and places in her article, but the psychologist recognized his treatment style, sued her, and received a huge cash award.

"I have their signed permissions," she said that day.

I snapped my fingers. "That's it!" That's what I had been trying to remember. She told me that she had given each person a copy of their particular case study and asked her or him to read it and to make any changes they chose to make it more accurate. She explained that she wanted to present each one of them as a case study to grad students at the university.

Had she gotten everyone to sign? I couldn't remember if she mentioned it, but I assumed she had. Surely Twila wouldn't have gone ahead without their written agreement. If she had their signatures, why would there be a problem? Perhaps one of them may have changed his or her mind. Was that possible?

Or maybe the case studies didn't contain the story of the person who murdered her. Maybe the murder was unrelated and something totally different.

What else is there? Why else would anyone hurt that wonderful saint of a woman?

19

I was still lying in my bunk when Betty came back into the cabin. I tried to think of anything else about Twila and her lectures. Nothing more came to me. The subject hadn't seemed all that important at the time.

Maybe it wasn't important. But if it wasn't, why the searching in her cabin? Why had she put a different cover on her own book? That seemed strange — almost as if she suspected someone. Had she been threatened? These were people she had chosen to travel with. Surely Twila was too astute to —

A knock at the door interrupted my thoughts. Before I could sit up, Betty was at the door and opened it. "Oh, did you come to escort us to breakfast?" she asked. "I'm not quite ready." She actually posed and flipped her hair with one hand. "But it will only take a second or two."

"I thought you had breakfast," I said to Betty.

"I did have a bite," she said, "but only a little toast and black coffee." She smiled at Burton. "A girl has to watch her figure, you know. But I could sit and enjoy another cup of coffee and listen to you talk."

"I think the dining room is closed by now," I said.

"Oh no, no," she said. "It should be, but it isn't. The others have just started to come in for a late breakfast — a very late breakfast." She draped one arm over the closet door as if posing for a photo shoot. I didn't know if that was her way of being cute. No, I decided she was definitely flirting with Burton. I had watched her bat her eyes a few times at men before.

'Uh, well, you see, I came —"

"I'm ready," I said. I grabbed my bag and hurried out before Betty had a chance to say anything more.

"See you later, Betty," Burton said.

He closed the door behind me.

"Thank you for saving me," Burton whispered once we were away from the cabin.

"Oh, did you need saving?"

"You didn't see how she came on to me?"

"Did she really? Oh, surely not," I said and hid my smile.

"Okay, Ms. Smart Mouth, you almost had me there."

"She was a bit obvious," I said and walked on ahead of him.

We sat down at the far corner of the first table, where I could see everyone who entered the room. Although there were no reserved places, by the second day, most of us had established our seating preferences. I purposely moved to a different place for each meal so that I could disrupt the orderliness of always sitting in the same place. I used to love it at church when someone would say, "Excuse me, but you're sitting in my pew." I would smile as innocently as I could and say, "Oh, you're welcome to sit here with me. There's plenty of room for all of us, don't you think?" They usually declined my invitation.

Okay, maybe that wasn't the best behavior. Twila once asked, "Is that an act of kindness? You make them uncomfortable. For some people, the one place where they can come and everything is as it should be is church. They like to sit in the same pew, and they want to see the same people each time."

She could have elaborated, but that was Twila. She knew she had made her point. I embraced her and thanked her. She was right, of course. Despite my inclinations, I didn't do it again. Even so, I thought of it almost every time I went to church. My actions were a little ahead of my good intentions.

I did it other places, however, because I wasn't yet a totally nice person. I was also still new in the Christian faith. At times, I resented being a believer. When I was on my own, I could make my decisions based on how I wanted to behave. Now I had to consult the Lord on everything.

In some ways, I'm a very, very slow learner.

20

We had barely gotten seated in the dining room before the waiter brought out our meals. He was also the Zodiac driver for the first boat that went out to Brown Bluff. Most of the crew, I observed, had more than one job aboard ship.

As usual, the food was absolutely delicious. They served the usual oatmeal, cold cereal, scrambled eggs, and bacon. But they always offered something a little unusual. Today it was strawberry crepes. I wondered why some first-class restaurant hadn't hired the chef.

Something else was interesting in the dining room. Every single one of those individuals paused and bowed their heads. Their lips moved, so I assume they thanked God for their food. I had never done that on my own. At one time I lived with a religious nut of an uncle who did geographic prayers before every meal — he prayed around the world in six minutes. (I timed him, and his shortest prayer was three minutes and forty-nine seconds. He must have been hungry that day.)

Captain Robert walked into our dining room. "Please continue to eat," he said. "I hope you have found the cuisine to your liking."

Several people said yes. One woman clapped, and that brought about a spurt of applause.

"I wish to make one announcement. I have nothing new to report to you." I half expected him to say something obvious, such as "Someone here killed Mrs. Belk." He didn't, but he did say, "I have spoken to each of you. You are all Americans, and we have been informed that delegates from your fine country will meet us at Ushuaia. They will continue the investigation."

"Is there nothing you can tell us?" I recognized Mickey Brewer's voice.

"I can tell you nothing —"

"Or you won't?"

"— at this point," he said as if Mickey hadn't interrupted him. "However, I have given unofficial permission to the Rev. Dr. James Burton and Dr. Julie West to act on my behalf until we reach our destination. If you know anything or have any suspicions, please to talk to them."

He gave us the pep talk about how delighted he was to have us and that in his eighteen years, this was the first time he had known of such a sad occasion. He bid us bon appétit and gave us a kind of salute before he left.

At first everyone around me whispered. Finally, Heather, who sat across from me and four seats down, asked, "Well, Julie, do you have any clues yet?"

"I'm waiting to find out what you know."

"Me? Why should I know anything?"

I smiled and focused on my eating. I had meant it as a smart-mouthed remark. As I reviewed the words in my head, I realized they hadn't come across as flip and cute.

The shock on her face made me wonder if I had spoken intuitively. *What if she does know something?*

It took about twenty minutes for us to get through the meal. Some stayed for coffee, but not many. Within another twenty minutes, only a handful of us remained in the dining room.

I got up, and Heather called my name softly. I looked up. She was sitting between Mickey Brewer and Donny Otis with Jon Friesen across from her. "Can I — can I talk to you for a second? Alone, I mean?" She turned and smiled at the three men. "Excuse me, guys."

"Sure, we can talk," I said. I stopped by Burton's chair — he sat at the other end of the same table. Betty sat across from him and was in the middle of a long story about how she had gotten lost for two hours in Amsterdam, or maybe it was Tel Aviv. Just to irritate her, I bent over and whispered in Burton's ear, "See you later."

He smiled. "Okay, I'll join you —"

Oh, now he wanted to play my game. "Give me ten minutes." I whispered in his ear, "The lounge."

"I'll be there."

"Come alone. Danger lurks."

He burst out laughing, and I hurried out of the room.

I walked slowly up a flight of stairs. Heather caught up with me and led me to her cabin. "I don't know how much good this is," she said, "but on Brown Bluff, I saw two people walking over toward a small hill or whatever you call it. It was just high enough to walk around and get out of sight. Maybe it's nothing, but . . . I thought you ought to know."

My intuition had been right, but I also sensed that wasn't everything. "What else

161

can you tell me?"

"They both wore blue — you know, like all of us."

"Yes, of course, but anything else?"

"One was taller. I know that's not very helpful, but one was taller, and — I assume it was a man — and he wore his life jacket."

"His life jacket? Are you sure?"

"I am. I know a few of us have done that because it's too much bother to take it off and put it back on. Still, it seemed odd."

It did seem odd, although I had noticed one or two people like that. "Anything else?"

"I'm quite sure the shorter one was Twila. You know she has a kind of limp."

"Yes, the long-lasting result from the accident years ago."

"That's right. Otherwise, I doubt if I would have noticed."

"Any other detail? I don't care how trivial it may seem. Please, think. Anything — even if it's only a slight detail, it could be important."

Heather thought, and finally she said, "The taller one — and I'm not good at heights — took her arm. I think that's what caught my attention. It was almost — well, rough. You know, aggressive?"

"Why didn't you say or do something?"

"I figured that if it was something serious,

she'd push away his grip or yell or something. Hey, come on now, who would have thought that any harm would have come to Twila?"

"You're right."

"Besides, the weather had already started to turn bad. Remember the wind and the first pelts of snow or sleet or whatever it was?"

I nodded and waited to see if she had anything else to add.

"That's it."

I stared at her. She really had told me nothing. "What do you mean? Surely you saw or heard —"

"No, that's it." She turned and went into her room.

"That's it?"

She said nothing more. I walked away feeling confused.

She wasn't some ditz who would just do something like that. In fact, in my limited knowledge of Heather Wilson, I would have called her a manipulator or an orchestrator. She seemed to constantly have things going on around her, but she remained in control. Maybe the term *control freak* was another apt description. Her calling me aside didn't make sense.

What is going on?

Was it possible that she wanted to talk to me for some other reason? She had very little to offer, and she could have said that in the group or at any time. Was it possible that she wanted to communicate a message to someone still in the dining room? To one of the three men? To someone else in the room?

"Stop, Julie," I said. "You've watched too many reruns of *Murder, She Wrote*."

"But what if — ?"

"You're not Jessica Fletcher, and this is no TV script."

As I slowly made my way to the lounge, I couldn't get past the idea that Heather did have some other purpose in mind. Was she trying to hint to someone? Was it possible she was trying to hint to the people around her or at another table that she had vital information? Was she merely trying to become the center of attention?

"Stop it, Julie!" I said.

"You're right. I'm becoming paranoid."

"Yes, you are."

"But still . . ."

21

He told me that no one had shown up for the first lecture on penguins. "We have already observed the chinstrap, rockhopper, gentoo —"

"Thank you for being conscientious about this, but our minds are elsewhere," I said.

"Yes, but of course, that must be so." He seemed genuinely apologetic.

"You're just being the captain. I understand."

He rewarded me with a smile. "I shall send someone to post a notice that the second lecture has been canceled."

"It's not because of you or the subject —"

"I am aware that you are correct," he said. "Would it not be difficult for anyone to sit in on a lecture about the difference between an Adélie penguin and a macaroni penguin when everyone thinks about the death of Mrs. Belk?"

Not trusting my voice, I nodded. I had

another of those unexpected moments of pain rush over me, and tears stung my eyes. If I had sensed the conversation would be difficult at the beginning, I would have been able to fortify myself.

I hurried on to the lounge and reached it before Burton. I chose a table and two chairs in the far corner. No one else was in the room, and I felt relieved. I stared out the window. The weather remained extremely bad, and there was little visibility. Still, it distracted me from my grief.

I didn't hear Burton come into the room, but I sensed his presence and turned my head.

He smiled at me and sat in the second chair.

"How do we go about this?" I asked. "I'm sure you're much better at this than I am."

He didn't answer, so I said, "You're so good at this. You make people feel at ease."

Burton chuckled before he said, "You've decided to revert to the airhead again."

"Sometimes it's fun to act naive."

"Right, so what is your plan?"

"I honestly don't have one, but I want to tell you about Heather." I told him what happened. I carefully kept everything factual.

"And you think she had some ulterior

purpose?"

I smiled. Yes, he caught it, too, but then, that's just one more reason I love the guy. He rarely misses anything.

"What do you think?" Again, that's a good psychological device to get the other person to talk.

"I've known Heather for about three years," he said. "She's not a bad person, and —"

"Okay, stop being the perfect Christian and sinless pastor —"

"You know I don't talk about parishioners —"

"This is murder, Burton. We both have lost —" I stopped, unable for a moment to go on. It was another unexpected stab of grief. My eyes clouded, and I bit my lip so I wouldn't cry.

He stared at me, and both of us remained silent. He clasped my right hand. "I miss her, too, you know."

I hugged him and held on. I think it was the action of a grieving parishioner, but it was probably also the action of a woman who loved the man in front of her and shared a mutual grief with him. I clung to him, and he held me tightly. He wasn't holding me as if I were a church member.

"Julie, I love you," he whispered. "I will

work through this — this problem of mine. Just don't pull away from me now. I loved Twila. I'm in deep emotional pain. I feel as if I've lost two of the people I love most." He put a hand under my chin and tilted my face toward his. He kissed me once, gently.

I didn't know if I should listen to my head or my heart.

His deep, deep blue eyes bored into mine. "Would you believe me if I said I missed you?" he asked. "I've missed you more than I've ever missed anyone."

I nodded.

He pulled me closer. His hands were in my hair, caressing the nape of my neck. My heart won the battle. I lost my self-control. We held each other for a long time. His arms were over my shoulders, and I held him, as we sometimes called it, by the lower rung. I loved the smell of Burton, even the cheap aftershave he always used. It was him, and he was there to share my deep inner pain. He kissed me again, and his cheeks were as wet as mine. I didn't pull back, but I clung to him.

I'm still awkward talking to God. But hardly aware of what I was doing, I silently thanked God for this man I loved and asked Him to heal both of us.

I prayed, I thought. *I actually prayed and I*

didn't even think about it. It just happened. That was a spiritual breakthrough for me, and I knew it. I had never prayed spontaneously before.

As Burton held me, calmness slowly penetrated my emotional pain. Something — something mystical — maybe miraculous — had taken place. I was at peace. In that moment, I realized how effective prayer can be. Peace slowly moved across my chest, and the overwhelming grief crept away.

He released me and took my face in both his hands and softly kissed my lips. I didn't resist. He pulled back, and I saw the tenderness in his eyes. We stood and held each other close for a long time. We didn't need words. In fact, I feared that if I said anything, it would spoil the serene moment we shared.

22

A few minutes later, Burton and I left the lounge, walking hand in hand to the now-empty theater. We discussed our strategy. We decided to call in each of those who had been passengers on the fourth Zodiac, one at a time.

We knew each other well enough that we didn't need verbal direction. Intuitively, I knew he would observe closely when I asked questions, and I would do the same for him. Our hope was to learn something new — anything that would give us a few clues toward solving the murder.

The one thing we didn't want was to have the group of them sitting together and sharing their perspectives with each other. On an episode of *NYPD* years ago, one of the policemen said it contaminated the evidence. That made sense, and I never forgot it.

We sat and I copied his list of the passengers in the fourth Zodiac, beginning with Jon Friesen, who came back in the third Zodiac. I pointed to his name. "Let's call him first."

"That's all right with me."

"As soon as we finish with him, we'll ask him to send in the next person on our list," I said, "and in this case it will be Heather."

He said nothing, but he gave me a thumbs-up.

"By doing it that way, you and I can have a couple of minutes alone between interviews, and we'll have the opportunity to compare our insights."

"Let the show begin," he said.

Burton went to get Jon, who told Burton that he would be up within a few minutes. When he finally came to the door, he paused, and I thought he was going to go into one of those bodybuilder poses. That wasn't quite what he did. He lifted his arms to the top of the door frame (his muscles bulged), and he seemed to be doing isometric exercises. He made no noise and waited until we made eye contact.

"I'm here, babe. Whenever you need me."

I decided to ignore that overly fresh tone.

"Sit down," Burton said in that quiet, soothing voice he uses so well.

"Sure thing, Burton," Jon said, but his

gaze never left my face.

"Tell us what you know about Twila's death."

"First, I didn't do it —"

"Did anyone accuse you?"

"I don't know — did they?" He had lost his swaggering pose. He turned to me. "Are you accusing me?"

"Let Burton ask the questions," I said.

"Go ahead. Ask." This time he looked at Burton. I sensed hostility in his voice.

"Tell us about you and Twila."

"She was a friend. A good friend. In fact, an exceptionally good friend."

"Really?" I interjected without thinking. "You gave me the impression that she had been your therapist for a few months, but you had no personal relationship with her."

Jon flashed me his best smile, and it probably worked on most women. He focused on my face as if nothing else in the world mattered. "I told you what you wanted to hear."

"What do you mean by that?"

"You liked me and you wanted me to talk, so I told you what you wanted to hear."

I changed my mind about him. I had first thought he was a borderline personality. Now I decided added to that he definitely had a few crossed wires. One thing to watch for in borderline personalities is how quickly they can jump from one mood to another. I wondered what medication he took — or neglected to take.

"Tell us about your friendship," Burton said.

"We were friends. We liked each other. We talked."

"About what?" Burton leaned slightly forward.

"You know, things. Movies, books, church stuff. God, sometimes."

"Did you like her?"

"Yeah, sure. Everybody liked Twila."

"Honestly, did you like her?" Burton said softly and in a quiet, intimate tone.

"Oh, she got heavy on my back about things, but yeah, she was all right."

"And you were one of her patients?"

"For a time."

"But you weren't seeing her as your therapist just prior to the cruise."

"Yeah. That's right, like I told Julie. I stopped."

"Want to tell us about it?" Burton asked.

"Not really, but I want to help, so I'll tell you anything you want." He told us that three years earlier, his wife had left him. She was his third wife, but she was the one he had really loved. He became angry and

173

trashed his estranged wife's house. The police arrested him, and the judge said that if he'd get psychiatric help, he would let him go.

"So that's when you started to go to Twila."

"Sure, why not? I was a church member — not your church. I was a member of a small church on Highway 138 called the Holy Family of God. My parents, now both dead, had been charter members at your church. They were gone, but Twila had been part of your church since I was a teen. Everyone I talked to said she was the best, so I went to her."

"Did she help?"

"I'm supposed to say yes because everybody thinks she was a wonder-worker."

23

Jon's response startled Burton, which was what he intended. The beginning of a smile appeared at the corners of his mouth.

"You're saying that Twila didn't help you?"

"Nah, she didn't. I mean, not much. But I got a lot of meds from her."

"Do they help?" I asked.

"When I take them, they sure do."

"Are you taking them now?" Burton asked.

Jon leaned back in his chair. "Uh, well, I started again today. See, I take Lexapro, twenty milligrams a day —"

"That's a high dose level," I said.

"That's what she said, too."

"What else do you take?" Burton asked. "I mean, *when* you take your meds?"

"I take Abilify —"

"You're bipolar?" I asked.

He shrugged. "Sometimes, I guess. I also take occasional lithium, which is supposed to make one side of my brain speak to the other." He looked straight at me and laughed as if we shared a private joke.

"Did Twila prescribe all three of them?"

"Can't remember."

"I'm sure she wouldn't have given you both Abilify and lithium — they're usually given for bipolar, but she wouldn't have prescribed both —"

"So I have more than one doctor."

Burton and I stared at each other.

He's stranger than I thought.

"Tell us about your trip to Brown Bluff," Burton said in an abrupt shift of topic.

"Do I start when I was born, or fast-forward to the day of her death, including what I ate for breakfast?"

"Just start with getting off the Zodiac when it landed."

"Sure, I can do that." He repeated what he had already told me. In fact, he repeated it almost word for word as if he had memorized his answers.

Burton kept switching from his account of the island to his medication and his feelings about Twila. Both of us became aware that when he gave us more than a smirky answer, it was the same wording each time, with almost no variation.

After perhaps fifteen minutes, Burton got

up, shook Jon's hand, and thanked him for coming. He asked Jon if he would send in Heather.

"Anything for you," he said. But he looked at me.

While we waited, Burton put his finger to his lips and nodded toward the door. I understood and sat in silence. Burton waited another few seconds and said loudly, "We'll see what Heather says."

A few seconds later the sound of light footsteps carried through the corridor. We stared at each other. Burton smiled as if to say, "Just as I thought."

Donny Otis tapped on the door. "I know you wanted Heather next, but — well, I'd like to get in here and get it over with. If you don't mind, I mean." He had a nervous habit of rubbing his left index finger and thumb together.

"Yes, of course it's all right," Burton said.

Donny stood quietly as if waiting for direction. I knew him by name, but I don't recall that we had ever spoken to each other. He was one of those people who came early and sat in the second row. At that church they have a ritual called the passing of the peace where people get up and shake hands with each other and say, "The peace of the

Lord Jesus Christ be with you." The other person is supposed to say, "And with you."

I mention that because Donny didn't participate. He sat in his pew, head down, and didn't act as if he knew anyone else was there. When we stood to sing, he opened his hymnbook, but from where I sat, and I always seemed to be several rows behind him, I don't think he opened his mouth. At the church they sometimes projected choruses on large screens. When they did that, he didn't look at the screens.

"Thanks for coming in," Burton said and extended his hand.

He shook Burton's hand. I extended mine, and he took it. His hand was about the deadest I had ever shaken.

"Tell us about you and Twila," I said. "How well did you know her?"

Donny stared blankly at me for perhaps half a minute. I guessed his age to be about forty-five or so. He had that male-pattern baldness with little hair on top, long sideburns, and a goatee. He was probably close to six feet tall, and he must have weighed 250 pounds. He was one of those men whose body was normal shaped, but he carried a watermelon-sized stomach in front of him.

"I did nothing to Twila. I wouldn't hurt

her. I truly would not hurt her." For such a large man, his voice was quite high-pitched and whiny.

"Do you feel someone has accused you?"

"I don't know," he said. He leaned forward and started the index finger–thumb thing again. "You might as well know — if someone hasn't already told you. I'm sure I'll be a suspect once we get back to the States."

"Why is that?"

"I tried to kill my wife. Twice."

"Tell us about that," I said in my most professional tone.

"The first time she made me so angry — no, Twila says — said — I shouldn't talk that way. It's my issue, not hers."

He paused, and I smiled to indicate I agreed.

"My wife touched places in me where I was vulnerable. Like we had no kids, and she always blamed me and said I wasn't man enough. That made me angry —" He looked at me imploringly. "See what I mean?"

"Go on."

"So one time I grabbed her by the throat. I probably would have killed her, but she kicked me, made me lose my grip, ran into the bedroom, and locked the door. She called the police."

"And what happened?"

"It happened twice. Both times she broke away from me, but —"

"But what?" Burton prompted.

"But the second time was the problem. I stabbed her."

"It was an act of violence," Burton said.

"That's why I'm sure I'll be a suspect."

"Go back to your situation. Did the police arrest you?"

Tears flooded his eyes. "They did. I mean, they did the second time."

"How were you charged?" I asked.

"My wife — Verna is her name — but she doesn't go to our church, which is one of our problems. That's been a big issue since —"

"I'm lost," Burton said. "You lost me between the arrest and Verna."

"It was like this. I was in the kitchen. I did all the cooking. Verna could do it, but she has defective taste buds or something. She can't even distinguish the difference between anise and oregano. I got tired of flavorless food and took over the cooking —"

"We got that part," I said. "What happened?"

"I was cooking meat loaf — that's my specialty — and ordinarily she didn't say

180

much, but this time she started complaining about my spending money for such a good cut of meat only to have it ground into hamburger. See what I mean? Defective taste buds. She couldn't tell the difference!"

"So what happened next?" I asked. It was going to take a long time to tell a short story.

"I grabbed the butcher knife. I mean, I suppose I did." He paused briefly and said, "No, no, that's not accurate. I had finished chopping the carrots and the cucumbers for the salad. I like my cucumbers small, like —"

"Did you stab her with the knife?"

"I guess I did."

"You guess? You don't know?"

"You're right. I do know." Just as he said that, he stopped the nervous rubbing of his fingers. "I did it. I cut her arm. It wasn't bad — just a nick. She grabbed a broom and fought me off. She jumped on me, scratched my face, and bit my fingers. I collapsed on the floor, and she called the police." He went on to explain that the court-appointed attorney negotiated a plea bargain. He wouldn't have to serve time if he agreed to see a therapist.

"So they sent you to Twila?"

"Oh no, no. You see, Verna wouldn't agree to my spending money for someone as good as Twila." He told us that he went to three different counseling centers and talked to two different pastors. "I didn't go to you, Burton, because — well, I was too ashamed. Don't feel offended —"

"I'm not offended. So when did you go to Twila?"

"When Verna realized that I wasn't getting any better — I mean, I didn't get violent, but she said the anger was still in my eyes —"

"And then you went to see Twila?"

"No. Verna went to see Twila and begged her to take me but for a lower fee. She agreed, and then I went to Twila." In long, verbose statements he started to describe the counseling he had gotten from others. By the end of his second visit to Twila, she had given him an antidepressant. "I'm not on it now," he said. "She wanted me to have it until I was better."

"Did Twila help you?"

"Oh yes, yes, she certainly did. That woman is — was wonderful. She helped me see where my aggression came from. Do you want to hear about that part?"

Burton shook his head. "Do you feel you're healed?"

"Twila wouldn't say it that way. She said I'm stabilized. I guess I am. I haven't had any violent episodes in more than two years."

"Sounds cured to me," Burton said.

"I feel I am, but Twila said —"

"We understand," I said.

He told us in lengthy detail that he and his wife stayed together. Both of them taught at a school about fifteen miles south of Riverdale in Fayetteville. His wife didn't like to travel and had turned down Twila's invitation for the cruise.

If he had been one of my clients, I would have let him talk, but I felt he had told us everything he could. Burton, ever the pastor, listened without interrupting.

He said he now spoke to young people at some group called Anger Anonymous.

"Oh yes!" I said. I realized I had read his case study, even though Twila had disguised it enough that most people wouldn't have made the connection. To cover up, I asked, "Did you know that Twila prepared lectures of her case studies?"

"Oh yes, yes, indeed." He became animated. "And I'm one of the cases. She chose me as an example of someone who had been misdiagnosed by others. She showed me a list of about maybe twenty things people need to look for —"

"You mean she showed you what she was

going to teach?"

"Sure she did. I signed a waiver, too."

"A waiver?" Burton asked. "What kind of waiver?"

"I gave her permission to tell my story. She said she didn't want to use real names, and I understood. I said I'd be glad to come to any of her lectures and answer questions. I want to be open about this and to help —"

"So you signed the — the waiver," Burton said. "Just one copy?"

"Oh no. Two. She kept one; I have one."

I had no questions. I wasn't surprised that Twila had asked him to sign, but I was amazed at the delight he took in being a case study.

Burton asked a number of questions, and Donny answered without hesitation. He had clearly relaxed.

Donny told us that shortly before getting off the Zodiac, Twila whispered to him, "You've remained stable. I'm proud of you."

Something about that statement didn't sound right. "Did she really say that to you? Those exact words?"

The startled look in his eyes made me know I was correct. He hung his head. "No, I told her I was doing great and that I felt the Lord had given me strength to overcome my angry impulses. She said she could tell, and then she said she was proud of me. She didn't say anything about my being stable." He apologized for lying to us.

He also said that he helped Twila get off the Zodiac. He took the life jacket from her and threw it on the ground next to his. He walked alone — which didn't surprise me. He said he noticed nothing and didn't realize that they were two people short on the return trip.

He had nothing more to add.

24

The third person to come in was Pat Borders. I knew him slightly. I remember that he wasn't a member of the church but attended regularly. He was a moderately successful real estate broker in the area. He was tall, quite thin, with sandy hair that just missed being red. He always looked malnourished to me, as if he needed a dozen good meals to make him look healthy.

"I'm surprised you came on the cruise," Burton said to him. I think those words were as much for my benefit as for Pat's.

"Yeah, well, I wanted to come. You see, Antarctica is the one place I've always wanted to visit." He explained that he was a world traveler, had been on all the other continents except this one. "This seemed like a good time to come."

"So Twila invited you for that reason?"

"Oh no, I begged her. And I insisted on paying my own way. You know Twila. She didn't like that, but I finally talked her into letting me come on the cruise."

He lied, and I couldn't figure out the reason. He was one of those people who constantly talked about what a great salesman he was — maybe that was part of being successful in his field.

"You paid your own way?" I asked.

"Okay, I didn't."

"That's what I thought."

"But I tried. I really tried." He looked away and finally said, "All right, the truth is, she didn't want me on this cruise. You know how I got on it? Only because Judson Knight broke his leg in a ski accident three weeks ago."

"So she already had the space filled and — ?" I asked.

"Yeah, that's right."

"Why didn't she want you?"

He shrugged.

"Were you a patient of Twila's?" Burton asked.

"Why would you think that?"

I smiled. "That's a good evasion." I decided to flatter his ego. "Very good answer, Pat."

He smiled in return.

"So were you a patient?"

"Yeah. Well, I had been. I wasn't currently

187

a patient."

"You felt you were cured?" Burton asked, and his eyes told me he knew the answer.

Pat shrugged a second time and looked away.

I became aware of the waves lashing against the ship. The rough waters had increased.

"No."

"Tell us about your situation."

"You can check her records when you get back. I was a patient for about three years." He held up his hands. "Okay, I play around with drugs, but I'm not an addict."

"But you use?"

"Sometimes. Yeah, now and then."

"Did Twila say you were an addict?"

"Oh yeah, sure, but she's a shrink — you know, that's how they're supposed to talk."

I smiled. "I'm a shrink."

"Yeah, but you're different, you know. You don't keep trying to make me say things like 'Hi, my name is Pat, and I'm an addict.' "

"Oh, so you mean you use, but —"

"I don't like being called an addict. It sounds demeaning, you know." He went on to say that he liked to consider himself an occasional user. "Or you can call me a recreational user."

He told us that he saw no cure for himself, and Twila had reluctantly stopped treating him.

"That's surprisingly insightful," I said. "Most ad— most users — aren't able to see that about themselves."

He shrugged and smiled. "Twila said I was bright."

"I'm sure you are."

"See, it's like this," Pat said. "I can go a full month without a fix — one time I went three months, and that was after I was with Twila. But something happens, and I do it again."

"What do you think happens?" I asked.

Pat shrugged.

"Why don't you tell me?" I said. "I'd like to understand."

"Whatever it takes for me to need to chill." He leaned forward as if he wanted to plead his case. "See, it's like this. I have this highly, highly intense job —"

"Real estate," I said. "I know, and I understand you're good at it."

"I'm the best. That's part of the problem. I am good. Last year my gross income was great —"

"But —"

"But doubts creep in, and I keep hearing myself ask, 'Can I reach that income level

189

again? How do I keep this up?' Then after a while —"

"You turn to drugs."

"Yeah, and I can't kick them."

"Do you want to?" I asked.

He stared at me for a long time before he shook his head. "Not really. That's why Twila wouldn't see me again."

"Did you like Twila?"

He hesitated even longer before he said, "I detested her."

25

"Twila said she could cure me! She promised me that I would be free, and she couldn't do that! She failed me!" Pat slammed his fist on the table. "She failed me."

"No good therapist would ever say that," I said. I moved closer so that my face was less than six inches from his. I could smell the coffee on his breath.

He blinked several times as if shocked that I would challenge his statement. "Well, not in so many words, but that's what she meant!"

"Really?"

"Okay, I *thought* she'd cure me. I — well, I want to lose the desire to — to, you know, to use. She couldn't cure me."

"So you hated her for that?"

"No, not for that."

"Not for that," I said. "But you did hate her."

"I didn't mean — no, I —"

"You hated her," Burton said in that calm voice again. "Just tell us why."

"She was so — so sanctimonious." He swore, cursed her name, and added, "She acted as if she was better than anybody else."

"You mean better than you?" Burton said.

"Okay, better than me. I detested her. Whenever she opened her mouth, it was always to talk about God. I hate God! I hated Twila!" He stood and lunged for Burton.

I grabbed his arm. He was strong, but I was able to hold him back.

Burton didn't flinch. He waited several seconds and grabbed Pat's throat. "Calm down. I'll release the pressure when you relax your body."

"What medication are you on?" I asked.

"Just a little something to raise my serotonin level, I think."

"Specifically?" I asked.

"I don't know. See, I threw a couple of handsful of, you know, prescription drugs into a vitamin bottle and brought it on the trip."

"So you don't know what you're taking?" I asked.

"No, and I'm sorry. Truly I'm sorry for

what's happened to Twila. I hated her, but I didn't want to kill her."

He seemed genuinely contrite. I released his arm and sat down.

"Sorry. Most of the time it works all right for me, but sometimes I get a little — well, bizarre. Instead of chilling, I get so angry I can't control myself."

Burton released his hold, and Pat sat still. Perspiration broke out on his forehead. "She wouldn't give me anything yesterday. I asked her, but she said she had nothing with her."

"And you searched her room?"

"I would have if I'd thought of it."

"One more question I have," I said. "Did you know she was going to use your case in a series of lectures?"

"Sure, I knew. That's how I persuaded her to let me come. I said I'd tear up my agreement." He smiled at me. "She made me sign a waiver."

"You read the piece about yourself." It was a statement, not a question.

"Yeah, sure. It wasn't very good — she made me look like a loser — but yeah, I signed."

"If I take you to the ship's doctor and ask him to give you a tranquilizer, would that help?" I didn't know if the doctor had anything, but it was worth trying.

"I'd like that," he said.

I took Pat to the ship's doctor, who not only gave him a shot of Valium but said he'd keep him in the bed in what he called the sick bay. "He can stay here until we land in Ushuaia."

I thanked him and went back to the theater. Burton had already brought in Betty Freeman, the next person on our list.

She was leaning across the table and staring into his eyes when I walked in. She glanced around and saw me but ignored me. "You know, Burton, I think you have the most beautiful blue eyes I've ever seen."

"God gave them to me."

Betty laughed. "That was very good. And that dark, curly hair." She reached over and touched his curls. "So soft. Not like most men. I have a little natural curl, but nothing like what you have. Whenever I see you behind the pulpit, I want to go up there and run my hands through your hair."

Burton smiled. "God gave me the hair, as well."

"If we're through with the eyes and hair," I said, "Betty, we need to ask you a few questions."

"Anything. Oh, anything, of course."

We talked to her for perhaps seven or eight

minutes. We learned nothing new. She had been on the fourth Zodiac. She didn't pay any attention to Twila. "Going over, I had a nice — really nice — conversation with Jon Friesen. He was complaining about not feeling well, but he was still nice to me. He's such a gentleman, you know. He lost his wife a few years ago, and he's so lonely —"

"Oh, right," I said.

"Did you talk to anyone else?" Burton hurriedly asked.

She couldn't remember. She didn't think so. She said she walked beside Donny and was with him most of the time.

"Most of the time?"

"Well, yes, except at one point — and I don't know where it was — he said he wanted to be alone, so I joined a group and walked around the gentoo penguins. I never get tired of looking at them. And there were two seals —"

"And you didn't talk to Donny again?"

"I did on the boat going back to the ship. Or I tried. He turned away from me and didn't say a word." She smiled before she said, "He did help me wash my boots."

I didn't think we would glean much more information from her. I made a note about Donny leaving her.

"Were you a patient of Twila's?" Burton asked.

"Client. She called us clients."

"Were you a client?" Burton asked.

She nodded.

"Do you mind telling us why she treated you?"

Betty told us a sad story about repeated sexual assault from her stepfather. She said she thought she had dealt with her issues, but her first husband beat her and she left him. Her second husband was an alcoholic, and she divorced him. "All of that happened before my twenty-fourth birthday. I haven't been in any serious relationship since then. That was five years ago. I'm twenty-nine now —"

"Did you know Twila used you as a case study?" Burton asked. "I read the account — even though she changed your name and cleverly disguised your identity."

"Of course I knew that," Betty said. "I never would have signed the waiver without reading it first."

After Betty left, Burton shook his head. "Sad, isn't it?"

"Yes, but what about Borders? Do you think he's capable?"

"Capable, yes. But —"

"But he seems erratic. He acts on the passion of the moment."

"That's my guess," he said. "Twila's murder may have been an act of passion, but —"

"But whoever killed her had to have thought far enough in advance to take a knife — or whatever it was — to the landing site."

"I don't think we want to rule out Pat Borders."

"Agreed," I said.

Burton smiled, caught himself, and did one of those polite coughs people do to cover up emotions.

Just then Heather tapped on the door, opened it, and came inside. She sat down. Before either of us had a chance to ask her a question, she said, "Yes, I was a patient of Twila's. Yes, I have a lot of problems — and I refuse to discuss them with you."

"That's fine," I said, although it wasn't really all right. "But did you know she used you as a case study?" I didn't know if that was true, but the others had all been subjects of her book.

"Of course I knew —"

"And you signed a waiver?"

"Not at first," she said.

"Because?"

"She made me look, well, like a — a tart."

197

"Are you?" I asked.

"That's insulting," she said. "Anyway, after she changed a couple more of the details, I signed it."

"Earlier you told me that you saw two people walking away —"

"Sure, and that's all I know." She said it again. She was very straightforward. I didn't like her attitude, but I had no reason to doubt anything she said.

Burton asked a number of questions, and she guardedly answered them. She said she liked Twila and that she had been a client for six or seven months. "She has helped me like myself so much more." She said she had felt like damaged goods when she started therapy, but Twila had helped raise her self-esteem. "She is — uh, she was so wonderful. She helped me so much. I could never thank her enough for all she did for me."

Those words were genuine. I could read Burton's face on that one and knew he agreed.

We learned nothing from her or from Mickey Brewer, who followed. Thomas Tomlinson came after him. Both men had been patients. Brewer had suffered from posttraumatic stress disorder (PTSD). He had been an employee of an American company selling a new brand of cola called Jolt in East Africa. A group of rebels had captured him and held him for ransom. When the company didn't immediately pay, his captors beat him and sent pictures of his bruised body to the company. He had been beaten five different times before they finally paid the ransom. When he returned, he threatened to sue the company, but they gave him a generous settlement. Months later the first symptoms of PTSD showed up. He reported acute anxiety. He tightened up, went into a panic, or began to perspire profusely whenever he heard loud noises. During heavy thunderstorms, he locked himself in a bathroom or closet — any small space that was dark. The slightest noise at night awakened him, and night sweats were so bad that he often had to change the bedding.

He explained — and we seemed to have to pull out every detail — that Twila had helped him to confront his memories. She had used a technique she called childhood regression, as well as some medication (of which he didn't recall the name).

"Twila helped. She really did. It took a long time — nearly four years — but now I sleep all through the night, and I don't take any medication." He said he had a dozen

Xanax in his room. He had not taken any so far.

When we asked him about the Zodiac and the walk on the island, he could add no information. He said he remembered talking with Shirley Brackett. Beyond that, he couldn't add anything.

Thomas Tomlinson was next. Before we asked, he told us, "You might as well know, I went to her because I had been arrested for DUI five times." He quickly added, "That was during my grad school days — before I began to teach." The only way he could get his license back was to go to a two-day DUI course. Afterward he also voluntarily went to see Twila. "I was determined to beat this."

She put him on Anabuse at first, but it made him sick even when he wasn't drinking. Once she prescribed Naltrexone — which was quite new at the time — it had done the trick for him.

He said his father had been an alcoholic, and so had his grandfather. He went on to say that Twila had helped him realize that he was one of those individuals who couldn't have a single drink of alcohol. "I tried cutting back to one drink, but that only started me. I couldn't stop drinking for at least two days and sometimes a full week."

Both of us listened to him. I was used to hearing such stories. That's how I make my living, but I wondered about Burton. He never showed any boredom or made any attempt to rush people. Yes, he would have made an excellent therapist.

"And did you sign a waiver so she could use your story?" I asked.

"Of course. I have no problem with that," Thomas said. "She wrote my case study objectively and correctly."

After that we interviewed Sue Downs. She was in her midthirties and had dull-looking ash blond hair and brown eyes. If hadn't been for her sloppy posture, she could have looked attractive. Of course, she'd have to do more than let her short hair hang straight and buy something other than those amorphous black dresses and black sweaters she favored.

She had also been a patient. She'd gone through a lengthy postpartum depression. Her baby had lived only four hours. She struggled with guilt. "I kept asking if God was punishing me for something I had done."

She admitted that she had "done sinful things" before her marriage, and she was sure that God was showing her she couldn't get away with them. Twila assured her that she wasn't being punished.

"In fact, Twila taught me about a God of love — something I hadn't really understood before. Until then I believed that God was always watching the bad things I did so He could punish me."

She spoke with such tenderness and with deep gratitude for Twila, it seemed obvious to both of us that she wasn't the kind who would have hurt anyone.

As we expected, she told us that she was one of the case studies. Burton nodded and winked at me. He had already figured that out. And yes, she had signed a statement that gave Twila complete freedom to do whatever she wanted with the case study.

"There is nothing I wouldn't do for that wonderful, wonderful woman."

She was so effusive I studied her closely. Sometimes it's the bit about overdoing the explanation. But she convinced us of her innocence with the last thing she said.

26

"I wanted to get pictures of me with a lot of penguins. Mark — that's my husband — adores studying pictures, and he makes beautiful albums for me." Sue's husband worked for the postal service and had been unable to get his vacation changed to go with her. "I don't think he really wanted to come anyway." She started telling about all the times she had begged him to travel, but he always said no. "But he's nice in that he doesn't mind my going without him."

"What about the pictures?" I asked.

"Oh yes, the pictures. Sorry," she said. "I have one of those 35mm cameras and I was having trouble getting the film threaded. It's an old camera — belonged to my father and —"

"And what about the camera?" I asked. I knew it would take an hour to get the information I wanted unless I kept intervening.

"Oh yes, that. Well, that nice Laird Hege came to my rescue. He was in the other boat, but he stayed with me until it was time for his Zodiac to start loading. Just then, Jeff walked up to where we were. He was so helpful. He stayed with me until we finished up the roll of film, and he put in a new roll for me. Wasn't that nice of him? I can hardly wait to see the pictures. He took at least one of me standing next to a sea lion. Well, of course, I don't mean next to one, but I was very quiet and stopped about five feet from the ugly old thing. He didn't make a move while I stood there. It's so funny to see them scoot across the ground when they want to go back to the sea and —"

"Was Jeff with you the whole time?" I asked.

She thought for a minute before she said, "No, actually, he wasn't. He joined Laird and me. I hadn't noticed him before because I was busy trying to get the best photo angles. And I had to step very carefully to avoid all the guano. It's so smelly and so —"

"And so Jeff just walked up to you."

"Yes, and he was so nice. I teased him because he didn't have on his life jacket —"

"No one had them on, did they?" I asked. "We all left them at the landing site."

"That's what I meant. But I had seen Jeff shortly after we got off. He had his on and started to walk away with somebody — I'm not sure who it was — and when he showed up later, without one, I teased him."

"What do you mean?"

"Jeff and I were classmates at North Clayton High School. Did you know that? I actually dated him twice, but he lost interest in me or something."

"About the teasing," I said and hoped my voice sounded soft.

"Oh, well, yes, that's why I mentioned North Clayton. We had a principal named Jim Steele, who didn't like Jeff. He was always calling him to tuck in his shirt or to tie his shoes or something."

"So?"

"Oh yes, well, he didn't have the life jacket on when he joined me, so I called out, 'Did Mr. Steele catch you and make you go back to the Zodiac and leave your life jacket?'

"He laughed and said something like, 'No, I noticed it before anyone caught me.' And then we laughed about old cue-ball Steele. He was bald, you see, and —"

"Yes, I see," I said. I looked at Burton and met his gaze. "How long were you and Laird together before Jeff came up?"

"I really don't know. It must have been

ten minutes. No, probably more like fifteen. But I don't know for sure. I know that by the time he came, the third Zodiac had started to load. Maybe someone else could be more precise about the time."

"Thanks, Sue," Burton said.

"I don't know if I had anything helpful to add. Did I?"

"Thanks," I said, not wanting to give her a direct answer. "We know how much you cared about Twila. It's nice to hear your experience. She was a wonderful woman."

"A saint," Sue said. "An absolutely true saint of God."

I got up and gave her a quick hug and guided her out the door. "Would you ask Jeff Adams to come in?"

Once Sue closed the door behind her, Burton said, "That was interesting." I knew he entertained the same thoughts that ran through my mind.

On a piece of paper I wrote Jeff's name. It wasn't that I needed to write it, but I wanted to keep notes. By the time we interviewed eleven people, I knew their stories would run together, and I wanted to keep them separate.

I wrote that he had left the Zodiac with the life preserver. When Sue saw him — which would have been at least ten to fifteen minutes later — he wasn't wearing the life jacket. I didn't know how much time Twila spent out of sight with the killer, but I figured ten minutes certainly would have been enough.

Burton said nothing, but I knew he had the same thought I had. Jeff had not been with Sue the whole time. He was no longer wearing his life jacket. That proved nothing, but it was the first significant thing we had learned.

27

Jeff Adams came in next. He was one of the half dozen or so people on the cruise I didn't know. Burton seemed to know him well and gave him an enthusiastic hug when he came into the room.

Jeff was about medium height and what I would call hefty — not fat, but what people used to call stout. He wore tight jeans, which made his legs seem even more bowed. He wore a tight T-shirt with a wool shirt slung carelessly over his right shoulder. He had thin hair, pulled severely back and tied in a ponytail. I was surprised that he wore only a T-shirt, because I thought it was always a little cool on the ship and wore either a hoodie or a sweater.

Jeff had tattoos on both arms. No words, only designs, but I didn't know what they were. From the color of them, they looked as if they had been there a long time. He wore a small gold earring in his right ear.

"I don't think I've met you," I said and extended my hand. "But I know who you are."

Jeff pumped my hand with such vigor, I felt as if I might not have circulation restored for an hour.

"I know who you are," he said. He had a wide, infectious grin. "I've seen your picture on Twila's desk."

I had forgotten about the picture. We had climbed Stone Mountain together in September. Despite her bad leg, she went all the way up to the top with me — although she was a little slow. We saw someone she knew who had a digital camera. He snapped the picture of us together and e-mailed it to both of us the next day. Twila had her copy printed and put in a frame on her desk.

"So you must have been one of Twila's clients," I said.

"Oh, absolutely. I was with her nearly three years, but she changed my life. I'm a different man today — totally, totally new and born again by the blood of the Lamb and sanctified by the atoning work of the Messiah Jesus." He had a preacher's loud voice, and I sensed he was just about ready to launch into a sermon.

"Are you a preacher?"

"A lay preacher, ma'am. How did you know?"

"Just a lucky guess." Burton's eyes said he would like to kick me, so I decided to behave.

"Yes, ma'am, I preach at the county jail every Saturday night and conduct a prayer meeting every Thursday night at the De-Kalb County —"

"I see," I said in my most noncommittal voice. "You and Burton seem to know each other. Tell me a little about yourself — I mean, other than your preaching tasks."

That may have been a mistake. *A little* turned out to be nearly half an hour of lurid detail about his criminal past. He also told me that he and Sue Downs had been in high school together. If he told us the truth, however, he had done more in those years than most criminals do in a lifetime. He described four cases of armed robbery and two tales of extortion, and in one of them he broke a man's legs. He had tried to kill someone — shot her three times — but the woman lived. He also had served county jail time on minor charges. He explained that he was not in prison today only because the police had made an illegal search.

"But that's where the grace of God began to flow into my sin-filled life and utter despair and brought me into deep repentance and —"

"What about Twila? How did she come into your life?"

"*That's* when she came into my life. She knew my sister, Ev Lewis, and at my sister's urging came to see me just before they released me." He told us (in what must have taken ten minutes) that Twila talked to him with a kind voice. Just before she left, she asked, "Jeff, don't you want God's peace? Aren't you tired of being alone in this world? Don't you want a friend who will love you no matter what you do?"

Jeff went into vivid detail of the power of her words. "It wasn't just her words, either, but the blessed and most holy magnitude of God's loving Holy Spirit behind them." It took him five minutes to tell his conversion story — and despite the redundancy and over-the-top language, it was a poignant tale.

I'll admit that once I got past his preacherly tones, his story fascinated me. He spoke with deep conviction, and the intensity of his eyes convinced me of his sincerity.

When he paused, I said, "Jeff, did you kill Twila?"

"Oh no, ma'am, I couldn't do that. I am no longer capable of such degradation and violence."

That's the short version. The real one would have taken a full page to tell. Everything about him said he spoke the truth.

But I wondered. I had met people in my practice who had done really terrible things, but they were able to convince themselves they had not done anything wrong. I wondered if Jeff was one of them.

Like the others, he had seen Twila's written account of his life and had approved it. "The only thing I didn't like was that she cut out a lot of the terrible things I did BC — before Christ."

"But you signed a permission form?"

"Yes, and in fact, she used my real name. I insisted." His chest seemed to puff out with pride.

I pulled my portion of the manuscript and skimmed through the pages. His story was chapter eight. I showed it to him.

"I'll bet it's the best of them."

"I'm sure it's the most violent —"

"Oh, that, too."

Jeff Adams left shortly after that. I was weary with talking to people. We still had to talk to nearly half of them. "So far, do you have any gut reaction?" I asked Burton.

"I want to keep my mind clear until we've interviewed them all."

"Good answer, Burton. But you do have some doubts already, don't you?"

"You know me too well." He laughed and added, "But that's all right. It works both ways, doesn't it? And you're wrong about Jeff."

"How did you know I had doubts?"

"I read your mind," he said. "No, that's not true. I know you well enough that I felt you had doubts."

"How so?" That's another good way to get an answer without saying anything.

"I think he's genuine."

"Because he preaches when he talks?"

"No, I believe him because of his eyes. His eyes don't lie."

He had me there. "Agreed," I said.

This time he laughed out loud. He was mentally tired from all the interrogation, and he laughed far too much for such a stupid comment. But I'll take any kind of positive response to my smart mouth.

"Someone has to be lying," he said.

"Or maybe . . . maybe we haven't asked the right questions." I have no idea why I said that. I mean, I didn't know at that moment.

28

Shirley Brackett came in next with her older brother, Frank. I felt as if I were the big, bad wolf preying on Little Red Riding Hood. Neither of them had married. Frank had been the janitor at the Methodist church for nearly forty years. Shirley was the senior librarian at the Riverdale library.

Shirley spoke openly and candidly when we asked them anything — but Frank said nothing.

Frank was probably in his late sixties, or maybe he was just one of those people who looks old at thirty. He had thick brown hair going white at the temples, but it was the wrinkled skin that made him look old. He had clear brown eyes, a long aristocratic nose, and generally handsome features. His salt-and-pepper mustache was large but well kept.

By contrast, I guessed Shirley to be at least twenty years younger. Frank was about my height, but she was small, about five two and perhaps slightly over a hundred pounds. She had the same brown hair without the streaks of white. She had delicate features, blue eyes that seemed to whisper gentleness. Her slender shoulders, thin wrists, long-fingered hands, and tiny waist gave the impression of fragility.

She seemed to be quiet in a way that could easily be called timidity, and perhaps it was. Her voice was soft, and it was easy to see why people paid little attention to her. Maybe there was nothing much to pay attention to. She wore a soft mauve wool jacket and matching slacks with a creamy white blouse that had a simple plum-colored bow at the throat.

I liked her softness and the way she looked directly at me when she spoke. "Were both of you together the whole time after you landed at Brown Bluff?" I asked.

"Of course we were," Shirley said. She leaned forward and said, "Frank retired this year." She mouthed the word *dementia.* "He's grown quite forgetful in recent days, so I spend more time with him." She said that after their return, Frank would spend each weekday at a senior adult day-care group.

Frank smiled if I looked at him, but most

of the time he said nothing. I don't know much about dementia, but I could see the deadness already starting to take over his eyes and his facial muscles. I revised my opinion of his age. His was probably closer to hers.

"Were either of you patients of Twila's?" Burton asked.

"As a matter of fact — I don't like saying that. It's such a cliché, isn't it? But yes, Frank was her patient for several years."

"What diagnosis? I mean, before — before his present condition?"

"Oh, he's schizophrenic. I keep him on his medication, and he functions fairly well. The problem, you see, is that after a few years, he has to change medication. That's where the stress comes in. He gets — well, let's say confused. When that happens, we have to change the medication. Twila was convinced that he built up an immunity to them. I believe she was correct."

Shirley offered to write a list of the medications Frank had taken, but Burton and I assured her it wasn't necessary.

"Frank never left you the whole time."

"I couldn't let him walk alone. He wants to pick up the penguins and pet them. He kneels down and tries to talk to them, and I have to remind him that he can't do that."

"Did you notice anything strange on the trip?"

"No . . . I don't think so. . . ."

"You hesitated," I said.

"*Strange* isn't exactly the word. Just something small — probably not worth mentioning."

"Try us," Burton said.

"Well, one thing that I thought was odd. I mean, it struck me as a bit peculiar."

"What was that?" This might take all night — and she might not have anything to say.

"I saw someone taking pictures — one of those digital cameras —"

"And that was odd because — ?"

"I wondered what the person was photographing. I mean, there was nothing really. Two members of our group in the blue suits walking all alone. Maybe it was for perspective or something. I don't mean to — well, I used to do a lot of picture taking when Frank and I traveled. I had the distinct feeling —"

"Go on," I said. I hoped I wouldn't have to beg her for every sentence.

"It just struck me as plain odd. It was as if the person followed the couple and seemed more interested in taking pictures of them — and she was maybe fifty feet behind them. I say *she*, but I couldn't swear it was a woman. But wouldn't that strike you as odd?"

"Did the two people turn around and wave or anything?"

"Probably not — oh, I don't know, but they seemed, well, they seemed unaware. That's part of what struck me as odd. I'm sure the person with the camera didn't yell at them. You know, if they were going to pose, they would have stopped or something. But I doubt if they knew —"

"Can you tell us anything about the two people?"

"They both wore blue." She laughed. "That wasn't much of a joke, was it?" She closed her eyes as if to visualize the scene. "I didn't pay that much attention. One was taller — oh, again, I suppose that's obvious. I mean, one of them would almost have to be taller than the —"

"Did either of them have on a life jacket?"

"Oh, the taller one." She thought for a minute. "Definitely the taller. And I assume it was a man —"

"Because he was taller."

"Well, yes, I suppose, but it wasn't that. He took the other person's arm — I'm not sure how to say it, but it was, uh, well, more like the gesture of a man than a woman." She leaned forward and said, "I write cozy mysteries, and I'm always observing the way people move."

"She's published two books," Burton said. "She's a gentle soul, but she likes to kill people in print."

"Oh yes, I use a pen name, too. My pen name is Mary LaMuth. I don't know if you've read —"

"That's very interesting." I don't read cozy mysteries, and neither do any of my friends, so her achievements meant nothing to me. "Back to the couple. Anything else you can tell us?"

"They seemed to want to get away from everyone else. Maybe that's obvious. Maybe it's just the mind of Mary LaMuth working, but I had the impression — it's only an impression, mind you — I had the impression that when he took her arm — and I assume it was a man — he was, well, not forcing her, exactly . . . urging, perhaps?"

"Anything else you can tell us?"

"Not really. My curiosity was piqued — after all, I am a writer, you know — and I probably would have watched or even followed the photographer. Just curiosity."

"Why didn't you?"

"Frank had gotten ahead of me. He spotted the penguins and started calling to them as if they were chickens. And I have to watch him carefully."

"Just two more questions," I said, and already I knew the answer to the first. "Did Twila plan to use Frank as one of her case studies?"

"Oh yes. He signed the waiver or permission slip — whatever she called it. And just to be sure, I insisted on signing as a witness. You know, when he gets worse — and he will — he has — he is — I mean —"

"The other question. Can you tell us anything about who was taking the pictures?"

"I'm sorry, but I can't. As I said, I had the distinct impression that it was a woman, but I can't recall why. There was something about her. . . ." She drifted into silence for several seconds. She shook her head slowly. "I know there was something about her, but it's just not coming to me right now."

She promised she would let us know if she remembered.

As soon as she was out of the room, Burton and I stared at each other. "Who took the pictures?" he asked.

"Would the pictures tell us something?"

29

"I did not kill Twila Belk!"

I looked up.

Heather slammed the door behind her. "Don't keep making everyone think I did it."

"What are you ranting about?"

"Ranting? Okay, call it what you want, but I'm angry — absolutely angry!" Her thick dark hair was parted in the middle and hung loose. She had looked beautiful before, but now she reminded me of an actress from the 1930s named Hedy Lamarr.

She slammed her purse on the table and sat down. "So let's get this clear right now. You've already questioned me once. All right? But ask whatever you want and let's get this over."

"Who thinks you killed Twila?"

"Everybody — well, I mean, several people."

"Why would they think that?"

"Because — because I got mad and said some stupid things to her, and several people heard me. That's why."

"What stupid things?" I asked before Burton could open his mouth. I'm quicker at things like that, and I love it when I jump in ahead of him. It also makes me feel bright.

"The day before, you know, before she died, I — well, I said some things."

"What?" I asked with an emphasis in my voice. "You might as well tell us. Or would you prefer we ask everyone else?"

"Oh no, no, please don't." Heather pulled a tissue from her purse and carefully wiped her eyes. She pulled out her compact and stared at herself in the mirror, brushing back a strand of raven-colored hair.

"Twila has, well, been after me for a while about something. I got tired of it."

"What did she bug you about?" Burton asked. He smiled, and I knew he jumped into the conversation to get ahead of me on that one.

"Okay, I smoke. Not a lot —"

"And — ?" Burton prompted.

"She said the cigarettes affected my health." Heather looked away. "She's also a medical doctor, you know. Well, before she takes a patient, she insists they get a physical — anyplace — and have the doctor send the results to her."

"And — ?" From the corner of my eye, I saw Burton's thumbs-up for pursuing that line. Heather didn't see it.

"Emphysema. I mean, I showed the first signs of it." She sighed. "It concerned her because, well, because I'm so young, you see."

Not that young. I didn't say the words out loud. I would have been willing to bet anyone that plastic surgery had kept that beautiful face beautiful at least ten years longer than it deserved. Or maybe I was still jealous.

"And she wanted you to quit smoking."

"She did. Like it was her own body. She was after me every time she caught me smoking."

"And — ?" I said again and winked at Burton.

"Okay, the day before. Right after we came back from our first landing —"

"King George Island," I said.

"Whatever. Whatever." She waved away my words as if they didn't matter. "I stopped for a cigarette on the deck. She came by. And you know how she is —"

"Suppose you tell me," I said in that soft, professional voice. I love it when I can practice all those phrases I learned in grad school.

"She cared about me. Yes, I know that, but I still resent it when people say and do things for my good. I know that she cared about my well-being. She didn't want me to ruin my health, and I know that. She loved me — okay, I got that message, as well."

"And the problem was?"

"I resented it. Maybe I shouldn't have, but I did. I mean, I know the cigarettes may eventually kill me. Who doesn't know *that?* I didn't need her to —"

"Or did you feel guilty?" Burton asked. His voice was soft and comforting.

Heather stared at him for a few seconds and nodded. "Yes, of course, I felt guilty, so I attacked. I was angry at her, and I yelled at her and told her to mind her own business. And she said I was really angry at myself."

"Was she correct?" I asked. "Were you?"

"Yes. And that made me even angrier. I have tried to quit. Eight times I've tried during the past three months. Honest, I've tried and — and I am going to get free. I mean, as soon as we get back —"

"So what did Twila say?"

"She saw me smoking and looked at me. Just that. Just a look. If she'd said some-

thing, I might have gotten really, really mad
—"

"So if she didn't say anything," I asked, "why were you upset?"

"Because she *didn't* say anything, that's why!" She looked around to make sure both of us got it. We nodded, and she said nothing. "So I yelled at her. I told her that if she didn't stay out of my personal life, I'd make her sorry."

"What did you mean by 'make her sorry'?" Burton asked.

"How should I know? I was upset. I didn't know she was coming up behind me, or I would have waited until she was gone before I lit up."

"And other people heard you? Is that the problem?" I asked.

"Yes, and they whisper among themselves."

"What do they say?"

"Its not so much what they say. It's — well, it's the way they look at me. I can tell what they're saying behind my back. I just know."

"You know because — ?"

"Because they act odd. They act extremely innocent as if they haven't said anything, but I know they've been talking about me." She brushed back her dark hair with her right hand. "Oh, I wish I had a cigarette now. It would calm my nerves."

She obviously showed signs of paranoia, but I waited to see if she had anything else to tell us.

"As a patient of Twila's, did you know she was going to use you as a case study?"

She sighed deeply. "We've been through this before, but okay, yes, I knew. Why wouldn't I know that?" I heard the anger in her voice.

"And you signed the consent form, didn't you?"

"No, I did not — not right then."

"Why?"

"She didn't think I was — well, curable. That's not the word she used, but that's what she meant."

"So that was the end?"

She shook her head, took out her compact, and carefully applied lipstick — which she didn't need — to those already bright red lips. "No, she disguised my identity and said no one could ever recognize me."

"Did you object then?"

"No, but after I signed, I decided not to see her again." Before either of us asked, she told us she had been a patient for a few months. Her company refused to keep paying, so Twila took her at five dollars a visit.

She said she had been raped as a teenager. "Twila never believed that. She always thought I made it up."

I wanted to ask, "Did you make it up?" but I restrained myself and got a nice smile from Burton.

She started to ramble about her treatments, and I was ready to cut her off until she said something about being involved with Jon Friesen.

"Really?" I asked.

"Oh yes. We had appointments right after each other. Every Tuesday and Thursday I came out of Twila's office at ten minutes to five. Twila always liked to have ten minutes between appointments to compose herself before the next client. Jon followed me at six. Almost every time when I came out, he was there, waiting for me, and we talked until she called him into her office."

"And what about you and Jon? Do you have a good relationship?" As I asked the question, I thought about his heavy-handed come-on to me.

"Oh, now, and that's — well, that's probably the reason I was really ticked off at Twila."

"You lost me there," Burton said.

"Well, Jon and I became, uh, I mean, *intimate.*" She smiled demurely. "We fell in

227

love. We were going to get married in April. But he broke it off. He broke it off, but she put him up to it."

"How did she do that?" That's another question I learned in grad school.

"She told him I wasn't healthy enough for a mature relationship."

"Did she say that to you?" I asked. Such a statement didn't seem like anything Twila would say.

"Well, naturally, not to me. She wouldn't dare."

"What did she say?"

"I mean, she didn't say it in those words, but I knew what she meant. And then — can you believe this? — she said I should tell him, tell Jon. Can you believe that? I was supposed to tell him that I was too messed up in my head."

"And naturally you resisted?" Burton used exactly the right tone, and she almost purred. "Did you?"

She shook her head. "Three days before we came on the cruise — three lousy days — he broke up with me. He just said we didn't have a healthy relationship. Now he won't talk to me — I mean, alone. When there are other people around — you know, like in the dining room — he's okay. But even then, sometimes he moves to the other side of the room when I come near him. No, I know what happened. Twila! She told him to break up with me because I'm — well, I'm emotionally delicate."

"Emotionally delicate?"

"So you honestly think Twila told him?" Burton jumped in with that soft tone.

"How else would Jon have found out?"

"You were a patient," Burton said.

"Client. Did you know she liked to call us clients?"

"Yes, he knows," I said, "but he forgets."

"So you hated Twila for that?" Burton asked.

"Hated her? I told her that if I owned a gun, I would shoot her fifty times."

"Did you stab her once?" I asked.

"Look, Twila may have thought I was on the wrong side of normal — and sometimes she might have been right — I don't know. But look at her files when you get back. I'm not violent. I yell and get mad, but my violence comes out in words."

"Oh?" That's always a safe word to use.

"If I were going to kill someone, I'd probably kill Jon!"

30

"I'm not clear on something," I said to Heather. "If Jon avoided you, how was it that you were on the Zodiac together?"

She smiled brightly. "Oh, that. Well, you see, when we prepared to land at Brown Bluff, I stood aside so no one paid any attention to me. I was there when the first Zodiac went out."

"And you waited for him to get into the fourth Zodiac?"

"At first I wondered if he had decided not to. Twila was the tenth person, and he was right behind her. So I took the last spot."

"Did you and Jon talk?"

"I tried. He turned his back on me."

"Did you talk to him at any time on the Zodiac or after you landed?"

"No, of course not. I decided to wipe that jerk out of my life — you know, Jon."

"So you didn't see Jon or Twila after the wet landing?"

"No, I don't know who got off first or last, and I didn't care. I didn't want to have anything to do with him again. Or with her, either."

Heather was lying. I knew it, but I couldn't figure out what she lied about. It didn't make sense. I stared at her.

"Okay, I did say something to Twila on the Zodiac."

"And — ?" Burton beat me to that one.

She began to play with invisible lint on her turquoise sweater. "I, uh, well, okay, okay, I asked her to get Jon and me back together."

"What did she say?"

"She only laughed, shook her head, and turned and started to talk to someone else. Jeff, I think, but I can't remember now. It was something about the pristine blue of the icebergs. Something like that."

"Twila laughed at you?" I knew that was a lie. "Twila laughed at you?"

"Laughed? Hmm, all right, maybe she didn't actually laugh, but I heard the mockery in her voice."

"Mockery?" I asked.

"Go on," Burton said and frowned at me.

"Twila said I don't always have a clear picture of reality — as if she knows everything. Okay, so I asked her to get Jon and

231

me back together. Maybe it wasn't a laugh. Maybe it — maybe she didn't. I *felt* like it was a laugh anyway. She said, 'It's out of my hands.' Out of her hands, huh? She made Jon break up with me, and it's out of her hands?"

"So what did you do?" Burton jumped in again before I could challenge her.

"We were almost at the landing. I waited for Twila. She seemed to be in no hurry and was the last one to get off the Zodiac. As soon as she was ashore, I helped her take off her life jacket. I dropped hers and mine with the others on the shore. 'Please,' I whispered to her.

" 'If Jon doesn't want to marry you, that's his decision.' Just that and she walked away from me."

"And — ?" I said it first this time.

"I joined a group — Shirley and Frank and maybe Thomas — I don't remember exactly."

"That was it?"

"I called her a . . . well, let's just say they were a lot of terrible names. Words I can't say with a preacher being present and all."

But you can say them to me, I thought.

She recounted her movements to us for a couple of minutes before she stood up and said, "I think Jon and I are going to get back together. You know, mutual grief and all that."

"Really?"

"Truly and really," she said and smiled. "He really does like me after all."

"Oh?" I asked, but she didn't respond.

We stared at each other, and she said, "I really have nothing more I want to say, so I think I'll leave."

Burton smiled and thanked her for coming.

Once I was sure she was gone, I turned to Burton. "She said one thing that bothered me —"

"The bit about the life jackets?"

"You picked it up, too?"

"I felt as if she wanted to give us a coded message," he said. "I didn't think it would do any good to ask her."

"I felt the same way," I said. "It was as if she threw a grenade at us and wanted to see if it would go off. There was something about the life jacket that she could tell us if —"

"But she won't."

"I know." That was part of her strange personality.

I had so many notes and much confusion going on inside my head. I knew — with that intuitive inner knowing — someone had lied. Maybe more than one.

"Someone knows who killed Twila," I said, more to myself than to Burton.

Burton looked quizzically at me and said, "Why would someone know and not tell?"

"I don't know the answer."

"But I agree with you." Burton's fingers drummed the table, and I knew he was trying to sort through everything we had heard. "Yes, someone is lying."

"One of them is Heather. But why? And about what?"

We decided to take a break for twenty minutes or so. I had a splitting headache. Maybe some of it was grief for Twila. I don't know. I decided to go back to my cabin for a Tylenol.

I had missed something. What was it? Something kept bothering me that I couldn't remember. It was some detail — something I had noticed, but I couldn't place it.

31

I walked slowly to my cabin, quite unaware of anything except my headache and trying to figure out what to do next. Somewhere there had to be an answer.

I sneaked into my cabin. And to my delighted surprise, Betty had fallen asleep with a book on her lap. I grabbed the Tylenol bottle and sneaked back out of the room. I walked down the hallway into the dining room where I could get water. I poured myself a glass of water and downed two pills.

"Need anything stronger?"

I turned around and saw that Jon Friesen stood in the doorway.

I smiled. I wondered if he would offer me an illegal drug. I put the small bottle in the pocket of my slacks and started to move past him, but I thought of Heather's comments.

"By the way, Jon, you came on to me

pretty strong."

"And I hope you're reconsidering."

"Why would I do that?"

He leaned closer to me. "Because I like you. I like you a lot."

"Really?"

"You know I do." He smiled, and I'd swear he flexed those biceps, but maybe I only imagined it.

"But I understand that you and Heather planned to get married."

"Not quite accurate. Heather planned to get married. I didn't."

"You mean you led her on?"

"No, I loved her, I truly did. Or maybe I only thought I did. She's very, very affectionate." He smiled, and this time I did see him flex his muscles. "I doubt that she's as affectionate as you would be — if you really tried."

I had gone as far down that strange path as I wanted. "But you broke off the relationship, right?"

Jon walked past me, picked up two cups, and poured coffee for himself and for me. I started to decline but thought better of it. I took the cup, and we sat at the first table.

"You want the story? Okay, it goes like this. I did love her — or maybe I only thought I loved her — I'm not sure. But she drove me crazy."

"In what way?"

"You want a list? That's easy. To begin with, she phoned me five or six times every day. I finally turned my cell on vibrate. I'd be in the middle of something, and the phone would ring. It would be that schizoid, and she'd say, 'I've been thinking about you. I've missed you.' She'd talk like that when she had called me only an hour earlier."

"Did you hang up?"

"No. I mean I didn't for a long time. When she called, she'd tell me how much she loved me and how much brightness I brought into her dark night. You know, heavy-duty gunk like that."

"And obviously you didn't like it."

"It was a burden. She constantly told me she loved me, and she would pout or cry if I didn't say I loved her."

"So you broke up?"

"Yeah, and that's why I'm available." He put his hand on mine. With my left hand I picked his up and moved it.

"I like the feel of your hand. Soft. Warm. I'll bet your heart is the same way: soft and warm."

"So, Jon, you broke up but you still came on the cruise?"

"I thought she would cancel. She said she

would. She'd go into all that melodrama about how life had no meaning without me."

"So that's why you came? You thought she wouldn't?"

"That and something else."

"What?"

"Do you really want to know?" He leaned forward so that our faces were only inches apart.

I didn't answer; I didn't blink; I waited.

"I knew you would be on the cruise. I like you — I think I love you —"

I laughed. "I believe you knew I would be on the cruise. I never made that a secret. But you didn't come because of me."

"You don't believe me?"

"Not for a fraction of a nanosecond."

"I'm not good enough for you?"

I didn't flinch, and I wasn't going to show him he made me uncomfortable, although he did. "It's my understanding that you and Heather have gotten back together again."

"Did she say that?"

"Yes."

He shrugged. "Okay, that's true. We're being discreet, but if you'd open up to me, I'd dump her —"

"Don't dump her for me."

I saw his fisted hands and the swollen veins in his neck. "I'm not good enough for you, am I? You think I'm trash because —"

"I'm in love with somebody else."

He stared at me for a long time before he said, "I thought that was over — you and Burton."

"Ask him." I got up and walked out of the room. He had frightened me. I didn't realize he was so capable of blowing up like that. But bipolars' emotions can jump from one extreme to another in seconds.

I decided I didn't want to be alone again with Jon.

32

As I hurried from the dining room, I tried to force myself to breathe slowly and deeply. I didn't accomplish that very well. Just then the ship rocked in the seas, and I had to grab the handrail to walk along the passageway. We were definitely in the Drake Passage.

For several seconds, a tiny spasm of dizziness came over me. *I can't get seasick now. Dear Lord, please don't let me get seasick.*

The dizziness left me, but the lurching of the ship didn't stop. It seemed to get worse.

Burton was in the theater when I arrived. His head was bent over. He was in such deep concentration that he didn't hear me come in. When I sat down, I startled him.

"I feel we're close — so close," he said, "and yet nothing makes any sense."

"Close to solving this?" I asked. "You're a lot more confident than I am."

"If only we could just get something

240

concrete about the person — probably a man — who walked off with Twila. We know he was wearing his life jacket then. We can only assume he came back alone."

"Except that no one saw him come back."

"Surely someone must have," Burton said. Unconsciously he pushed back that gorgeous lock of dark curls. He smiled, but it was a tired expression.

"Let's call it a night," I said.

"It's not even noon yet," he said.

I looked at my watch. It was exactly 11:45.

We stood up and faced each other. I know he wanted to kiss me. Okay, I wanted him to kiss me, but I couldn't. If he took me in his arms, I'd lose my resolve about having him make things right first.

He must have read my face because he said, "I won't kiss you — not this time." We walked down the passageway together, then he went up a flight of stairs to his room and I started down one flight to reach mine.

I went into the room, and the ship rocked wildly in the waves. Betty had left the room, and I was glad that I wouldn't have to mumble answers. I got into bed — still dressed. I pulled my luggage inside the bunk, made my body the shape of a banana, and put books and luggage on both sides of me. I had learned that as a trick when I had gone on a cruise with my late husband, Dana Macie.

I don't remember going to sleep, so I must have dozed off pretty fast. But I also awakened with a start. I have no idea what awakened me, but I was fully alert. I know myself well enough to realize that when I'm that alert, there is no going back to sleep.

I lay in my banana position for several minutes. I prayed. I honestly prayed for divine guidance. It's not supposed to be difficult to pray — or at least the books I've read seem to say that. But it was for me. *Who am I that the God of the universe wants to listen to my petty cries?*

I smiled to myself. I had asked Twila that question. She said that was how God's grace worked. And God cares about every single person. I believed her and I had started to pray — not as much as I knew Burton did. I had decided that I would set aside a few minutes when I first awakened and talk to God. I still planned to but had never felt good enough, despite what Twila had said.

But then — right then — I *knew* I could pray and that God would hear me. It was almost a giddy experience. *God will listen! To me!* I talked to God right then. I poured out my concern about finding the killer. I asked God to show me or Burton or both of us what to do.

I had no answer, but I had peace.

I stuck my arm out of the covers and held it toward the light. It was 2:37 p.m. I had slept through lunch. The sea felt even more ferocious than before.

Betty moaned. If she was following the same pattern going across the Drake Passage as she had before, then she had taken two seasick tablets. I suspected she still was feeling somewhat queasy.

Finally, I got out of bed, put my shoes back on, and tiptoed out of the room. I thought perhaps a cup of tea would help. According to my British friends, tea is the cure for everything.

If the trip back was anything like our trip going to Antarctica, we'd have a number of seasick people, including some of those who had taken medication.

I held on to the railings because of the pitch of the ship. Even though I was holding on, a sudden rocking of the ship threw off my center of balance.

Just then I heard a voice. It was a woman's voice, and she was shouting. I couldn't make out most of what she yelled, but I heard the word *camera* several times, as well as the word *picture.*

The other voice, a man's, was too low for me to be sure of, but I think I heard the word *observant.*

A shrill scream filled my ears. Despite the noise of the waves striking the hull of the ship, I heard that scream.

Foolishly, I raced forward and left the handrail.

I reached the top of the stairs, but in my haste, my clasp on the railing wasn't strong enough. Another wave hit. I lost my balance and pitched forward. I screamed — it just came out. I tumbled all the way down to the bottom of the passageway, perhaps ten or twelve steps.

Once the shock was over, I got up slowly. I had landed on my right arm and right side. I had probably bruised my arm, but nothing was broken. I got up cautiously and moved as quickly as I could to the area where I had heard the voices.

"Listen, Julie," I said aloud to myself, "just because you heard a few words, don't go jumping to conclusions."

"You're right," I said. "But still —"

"Still, what?"

"Something about the tone of her voice. She sounded afraid. Maybe almost hysterical —"

"Oh sure, so that means the conversation

has relevance to this situation. You think everything that's spoken by anyone refers to this —"

"Right," I said and added, "but still . . ."

I kept going. I wasn't sure where I was going, but I knew the general direction.

Then I saw her.

My initial impression, of course, was that she had fallen. She lay facedown on the carpeted floor. Blood was already beginning to seep from her body. I knew immediately who it was.

33

I recognized Heather's turquoise sweater and that inky black hair. She had fallen forward. A pool of blood had seeped onto the carpeted floor.

I touched her gently and tried to turn her over. Her eyes fluttered, and she tried to say something, but I couldn't hear it. Her eyes glazed and all life was gone.

Stab wounds around her neck made my stomach roil.

"Oh, dear God, not another life taken." As I held her, not knowing what to do, I thought of the two times Burton and I had been involved in murder cases. Both had started with a murder, and there was a second one — someone who had witnessed the killing or who held a vital clue toward solving it.

I hadn't liked Heather very much, but a wave of sadness came over me and tears filled my eyes. Perhaps I was really mourning for Twila. I know only that I hugged the lifeless body and sobbed.

I was too distraught to be fully aware of what happened during the next few minutes. Sue Downs came out of her cabin — she later said it was to get more seasick medicine. She saw me holding Heather's body and screamed.

I calmed her down by talking slowly and softly and told her to go to the navigation bridge and tell the captain. Minutes later, two of the seamen came. They gently lifted Heather's body, covered her in some kind of tarp, and took her away. A stewardess came and wiped away as much blood as possible and covered the blood with a small rug, which was almost the same color as the carpet. Her blood had streaked the front of my clothes.

It's fuzzy in my mind, but I know that I asked someone who came by — maybe it was Jon or Mickey — to call Burton. He came soon after that. I had been so caught up in the trauma of the situation that my mind had been unable to function properly.

Burton put his arm around my shoulders and led me to the dining room. He sat down next to me. He held my hand. "We've been through this kind of thing before," he said.

"People see something, and the killer takes them out of the way."

Then I remembered what had been lurking in the back of my mind. "I know why she was killed — I mean, I think I do." Before he asked anything, I said, "There was something tickling the back of my memory. Now — maybe too late — I know what it was."

I stared at him. "A camera. Heather had one of those tiny digital cameras and snapped pictures all the time."

"You know, I do remember that."

He told me to wait, and he ran to her room. Minutes later, he returned. "No camera. Sue is her roommate and she'll look more carefully, but neither of us found her digital camera. Sue said she never left the cabin without it." He said he had also checked with the ship's doctor, who confirmed there was no camera on her person.

It was obvious to both of us what that meant. Heather had seen someone walk away with Twila and had probably photographed them.

"Remember what Shirley said? That's what bothered me. She referred to the woman who watched them — and who took pictures. That had to have been Heather."

"We can't prove it, of course," he said,

"but it makes sense to me."

"So Twila's killer was probably being blackmailed." I told him about hearing the voices and the scream.

"That fits." He began to ponder the time frame. "By then the first two Zodiacs had gone, and maybe ten minutes afterward, the third one left."

"Let's not even think along that line," I said. "Too many suspects again."

Burton stared into my eyes. "I haven't napped. I've spent the whole time in prayer. I don't know anything, but I sense, I truly sense, that God will help us find the killer before we dock at Ushuaia."

Please God, I prayed silently. *Please hear his prayer. And mine, too, if You don't mind.*

34

Burton and I met shortly after dinner. He said he had finished his half of the book. I had also finished mine. He walked me to my cabin, and we exchanged halves.

"Two of the accounts are extremely interesting. I don't know if it means anything, but if we knew who they were, it might help. But without any identity —"

"I'm sure we can get the key from Twila's file once we get back to Atlanta."

"But we may also lose the impetus and any chance to find who killed both of them."

He didn't have to say it. Both of us assumed the same person who killed Twila had also killed Heather.

"I had a thought —" I was a little embarrassed. "Do you think God sometimes puts thoughts into our heads? Please don't laugh. You know I'm still new at this Christianity —"

Burton took my hand. "I'm not laughing.

And yes, I believe the Lord speaks to us. If not, why do we ask for guidance?"

"I mean, it's not a solution or anything —"

"It's all right." This time he gave me what I call the sideways embrace — like two friends who stand next to each other. His arm around my shoulder comforted me.

"Well, it's just that I keep thinking about the book — the lectures —"

"And — ?"

I laughed this time. "And — to repeat your word — maybe the killer isn't in the book but doesn't know he isn't. So he still tried to steal it —"

"Unless that person already has what he wanted."

"That's a possibility," I said. "Okay, I prayed, and here's what came to me, whether it's my subconscious working overtime or —"

"It's all right."

"But, darling —"

"You called me darling," he said.

"Yes, I did."

"Did you — were you aware — ?"

"I'm aware of my words, but, you know, sometimes words just slip out."

"Let them slip out as often as you like. *Darling.*"

251

"Meanwhile, back in Antarctica, let's assume that the person didn't find what he wanted — that is, he wanted the manuscript — he may not have known what it looked like."

"He wouldn't have known what it looked like," Burton said. "That is, assuming the book is what he wanted."

"You're probably right. If he had known it was a book, he would have riffled through the six books in Twila's briefcase."

Burton thought for a few seconds before he said, "So he probably doesn't know Twila had the case studies bound."

"I feel — oh, Burton, is it okay to say that? I feel God is going to help us figure this out."

"Yes, yes, it's fine. I don't have that feeling, but I hope you're correct."

Burton and I talked for almost an hour, going over our notes and our impressions. We were more convinced than ever that the killer was one of the people on the fourth Zodiac.

At breakfast the next morning, Captain Robert announced the death of Heather Wilson. Everyone seemed shocked.

"Oh dear, is it something we should fear?" Shirley asked. "Is there a killer loose who —?" She stopped and said quietly to me, "There I go in my Mary LaMuth mind-set."

"Doesn't anyone know anything?" asked Mickey. "How many more people will die before we get back to Ushuaia?"

"Do you suppose we ought to, you know, stay in twos?" Betty Freeman asked. "If one of you nice gentlemen wanted to guard us defenseless females, I, at least would appreciate it."

"After all, both people who died were women," Sue Downs said.

"I'll be your escort," Donny said.

Several other men echoed his words.

Burton stood up and waited until everyone stopped talking. "I don't think anyone else needs to be afraid. I'm quite sure there will be no more deaths."

I stood next to him and said, "I think it's time we told you what little we know."

Burton stared at me as if to ask, "Are you out of your mind?"

I stared back and shrugged just the way he does. I love communicating with him when we don't have to use words.

"The captain gave Burton and me un-official permission to work on finding the killer —"

"And you've brought about a second

murder," Donny said.

"That's not fair!" Jeff yelled. "They didn't kill Heather."

"You're right, Jeff," I said. "Heather would have been killed even if we hadn't gotten involved."

Now I had their attention.

"We know one thing we can tell you: Twila planned to do a series of lectures at Clayton University, and she had written twenty-one case studies. We think the killer wanted to get the material and destroy it."

"And did the person succeed?" Thomas asked.

"No," Burton said. He held up his pages. "This is half of the manuscript on which she worked."

"I have the other half," I said.

"We're still reading it," Burton said.

"What kind of case studies?" someone asked. I don't know who asked, because it came from behind me.

"I can only say this much — and I'm sure it's obvious to all of you. We have good reason to believe these pages will implicate someone on this cruise." As I said the words, I could hear Jessica Fletcher on *Murder, She Wrote* say the same thing. In fact, I could probably go back to those old black-and-white Perry Mason cases where he often said something just as silly.

"Is that all you're going to tell us?" Jon Friesen asked.

"For now." I have no idea why I answered that way. I think I was trying to imply that we had information we weren't ready to divulge.

Despite all the questions people wanted us to answer, Burton and I left the room. "This is beginning to sound like some TV plot," I said. "We announce the evidence and set a trap for the killer to come and try to steal the book, and we've got him."

Burton laughed.

"Do people really think that way?" I asked.

"Only in movies and books. Only in fiction."

35

I decided to go to the lounge. A lecture was scheduled for ten o'clock in the theater. I couldn't have concentrated on it anyway. I wasn't sure where Burton went.

After getting a glass of water, I sat in the corner and read through the chapters. In spite of my PhD in psychology, I have to admit I learned from Twila. She was insightful and obviously saw things that I probably wouldn't have picked up.

I felt my eyes starting to water again, and I resolutely fought the tears. I could grieve later. This was our last full day on board.

Perhaps twenty minutes later, I heard whistling and looked up. Larry Dean Yoke came into the room. I knew him slightly, and he usually gave me a cheerful salute.

"I finally feel good," he said. "I had a good night. I took a seasick pill and slept fine." Larry Dean, maybe fifty years old, looked like a big farm boy who had awakened inside the wrong house and been forced to clothe himself in Yves Saint Laurent gear. His brown hair was combed straight back, and he had long gray sideburns. Despite his expensive clothes — and they shouted money — his square face and plain features looked out of place.

Larry Dean said he had decided to bypass the lecture and find something to read instead. He spotted a book called *With Byrd at the Bottom of the World* by Norman Vaughan. He picked it up and started telling me what a fan he had been of Byrd and his historic air flight over the South Pole in 1929. He admitted he had read the book years ago, but he liked it and since it was here, he decided he would read it again.

He came over and started to sit down but saw I was busy. "Oh, guess you don't want company."

I shook my head.

He leaned over and read enough to see what I was reading. "I'm in that book. I suppose you know that."

"You're one of the twenty-one?"

"Absolutely. I'm the male with the multiple-personality disorder." He beamed as if proud of his past condition. "I'm fine now. Occasionally, I get slightly, well, strange, but not often."

"Do you know anything about Twila's death?"

"Nope. Sorry. I liked her. I really did. It's because of her that I first went to church and eventually became a serious Christian." For another minute or two, he went into the details of his conversion story. He paused abruptly and said, "Sorry. You didn't ask about all that, did you?"

Rather than answer, I asked, "Do you know anything that would shed any light on this?"

He shook his head. "I was on the first Zodiac. We left maybe ten minutes after the fourth one landed. I never went near the fourth one or talked to anyone." He went to great length to tell me the people he had been talking to. And he took a lot of pictures of the Zodiacs as they came in. "I like those little things."

"So you read what Twila said about you?"

"She didn't have anything to hide from us. She talked to each of us and explained what she was going to do. She said that by telling our story and the way she had intervened, she could help professionals treat others."

"Yes, yes, that's excellent," I said.

"I feel honored to have been in the book. In fact, I was one of the last ones to go into it." He took my copy and turned to the last chapter. "See, that's me." He pointed to MEZ.

"But she doesn't identify the people —"

"Well, not really. I mean, she does in her own coded way."

"What do you mean?"

"I gave her a simple system — I mean, really simple. She called it a great memory retrieval system."

I must have looked totally puzzled, because I had no idea what he meant.

"It's easy and obvious. My name is Larry Dean Yoke. That makes my initials LDY. Right?"

"Of course."

"So instead of using those initials, she took the *next* letter in the alphabet. Instead of *L* for Larry she used *M.* Simple, huh?"

"Yes, it is. So MEZ moved back one letter makes it LDY."

"That's it. You still can't identify everyone, but those of us who were patients could identify each other. And that was part of the permission form."

"What do you mean?"

"Well, Twila didn't think it ought to be a secret among her patients — her clients. She had a party every couple of months for all of us — if we wanted to come. Nice

259

party. Good food."

"You mean like an AA meeting or — ?"

"Not that formal. But we talked a little about ourselves. So we pretty well knew each other. Most of us thought it was fun." He abruptly stopped and pointed to the chapter I was reading. That's Pat Borders. He's Pat Robert Borders and that becomes RSC. We used to laugh about each other's problems."

"And everyone was cool with that?" I asked.

"Cool? We loved it. She also had a contract with one of the university presses — University of Iowa. Or maybe it was Illinois."

"By any chance, do you know if all twenty-one people in the book are on this cruise?"

"Absolutely. That's one of the reasons we came. It was her way to thank us. She said she learned so much from treating us."

"And the rest of us on the cruise are friends, right?"

"Yeah, maybe seven or eight like you."

I stared at Larry Dean for quite a while. I had made a list of the three-letter codes of my half of the manuscript. I went down the list. Larry Dean was quick. He called out their names before I did.

I had the names of all twenty-one.

"Thanks, Larry Dean. Twila would have

loved you for what you just told me."

"You mean I helped? I don't see how, but I'm glad if I could do anything." He started into a story in which he told me how Twila had saved his sanity and had made him a more solid believer in God.

"Forgive me for interrupting you —"

"Oh, that's all right," he said. "You have something more important to do than listen to me."

"It's not that I don't want to hear," I said as I gathered up my materials. "I have to see Burton."

He winked. "Naturally."

I hurried out of the lounge.

Now I know.

36

At first I couldn't find Burton. He wasn't in his cabin, and I knew he wouldn't have gone to the theater. I went back to the dining room and didn't see him.

"Julie."

I whirled around. He had been sitting in a corner with no light on.

"I know, Burton! I know who did it."

He listened to my long explanation of the conversation with Larry Dean. I did that on purpose and strung out the explanation as long as I could. I love to make him eager and expected him to say wearily, "And what's the point?" The rat! He never did. I looked at his face and I understood. He knew what I was doing, and he was willing to wait me out.

"So do you want to know?" I asked.

"Yes, and I will as soon as you decide to share your information."

Impulsively I pecked him on the cheek.

Only after I had done that did I realize what I had done. I felt my face flush.

"It's okay, Julie," he said. "I won't take the kiss personally." He said the words with no facial expression, but I knew he was laughing at me.

"Okay, here it is." I showed him my list of four columns. Their names were listed first; then their initials in Twila's code; and third, their true initials, which matched the first column. My final column was a brief note of the problem the person faced.

"So now at least we know the identities of all twenty-one people," I said.

He studied the list carefully. "And, of course, each one is on the cruise."

"That was part of Twila's way of thanking them for their help."

"And you think you know who did it?"

"Absolutely," I said with a little hint of pride. I felt great. Burton is usually a step ahead of me, but not on this one. "Of course, I can't prove it —"

"So now you want my help to bring out the evidence to convict the guilty one."

He's bright, and I never have to explain anything to him twice.

"So tell me."

"First, the killer isn't one of the people in the book of lectures."

"He's not? Then why — ?" I loved the look of confusion on his face. It was worth stringing out the story just to see that.

I didn't answer, but I did smirk. I love doing that.

"So you want the great dramatic ending to this, do you?" he said. "We get them all in the dining room. You make your grand explanation, point to the guilty one, and proclaim, 'You did it.' And that person cries out a confession —"

"Not quite that simple," I said.

"Life rarely is."

"Let me try this," I said. I still hadn't told him who the guilty person was, and I wanted to wait until he begged me.

"At last," he said and smiled. He had figured out my game.

"He was one of those who never made progress in therapy. Don't you get it?"

"He wasn't in the book because — ?"

"Because he was *too* sick — *too* mentally ill. He wasn't a good case study." I didn't need to explain to Burton that she chose the twenty-one clients because she felt her students could learn from the cases. Not all of the subjects ended up normal or cured (a word we professionals don't use). But she wouldn't have made a case study of someone who remained stuck for years and hadn't moved on.

"I hate to admit it, but this time you're way ahead of me." He scratched the back of his head as he skimmed the list. "You'll have to convince me that the killer isn't on the list."

"The best argument," I said, "is the most obvious. Every one of the people — all twenty-one of them — gave their consent."

"Have you asked all of them?"

"No, and I don't need to do that. I can if you like, but you're missing the obvious."

"No, you're missing the obvious. Until you know —"

"Try this, then. I've spoken to everyone on the fourth Zodiac. All of them have said they signed off —"

"Right. Okay, for now. I agree with you that —"

"That they had nothing to be afraid of. She gave each of them a copy of the chapter in which their case is discussed."

"Oh, I get it!"

I smiled. All right, I smirked again. I could get good at that expression.

"So the killer *assumed* she had written —"

"You were a little slow on this one, Burton, but that's exactly right."

"It makes perfect sense," he said. "So the

killer didn't sign —"

"And —" I paused for dramatic effect and just one more smirk. "He didn't know he wasn't in the book, so —"

"So he searched the room to find it —"

"Now that makes sense, doesn't it?"

"It's worth exploring." I knew he agreed with me completely, but he wasn't going to let me score too many points. "Let's be really sure," he said. "Let's compare the list to the eleven other people in the Zodiac with Twila."

I had already done that, but I wanted him convinced. All of those who came back on the Zodiac were on the list.

"No, no, I'm sure who killed Twila, and he also killed Heather —"

"Because she saw him do it?"

"No, but she knew."

He stared at me for a long time. "You lead," he said. "I'm with you all the way."

As we both stood up, I said, "I can't prove this yet, but there is a chance I can later."

"We have nothing to lose, do we?"

"Only that we'll enrage the wrong person and let the guilty one get away."

We started to walk, and I put my hand against his chest. "Uh, I, uh, want you to do something. Please."

Burton stared quizzically at me.

"Will you pray for God to help us? I mean, that's all right, isn't it?"

"Here's my rule," he said. "If anything is big enough to concern you, it's big enough to concern God."

"I like that," I said. "That's a good rule."

Burton took both of my hands in his and prayed. The words flowed so easily from him. My uncle's prayers had sounded more like commands or sermons. I loved to listen to the way Burton prayed.

When he finished, I said, "You talk — well, as if you're conversing with a friend. It sounds so natural."

Burton beamed. "Jesus Christ *is* a friend. My best and truest friend."

37

Burton and I went to find Captain Robert. It took about ten minutes for me to explain everything to him. He didn't understand about Twila's lectures and why permission was important, but he didn't demand any further explanation. I finished and Burton clarified a few minor points for him. I didn't explain to him and I hadn't told Burton, but I was positive I knew the killer's identity. It simply made sense to me.

"You are convinced that you know the killer's identity?" Burton asked.

"No," I said. "I'm not positive, but I think so." I turned to the captain and said, "If you'll help us, we'll soon find out if I'm correct."

He pondered the situation for perhaps half a minute. "I have no objections whatsoever. My concern must always be about the comfort of our passengers."

I started to say, "I read that in your

brochure." Instead, I saw the frown on Burton's face and said, "I'm sure that's true."

"We live in — what do you call it — a litigious world?"

"We certainly do," I said. "But I don't think that is a problem."

"You see, Captain, I know every passenger on this ship," Burton said. "Except for eight of them, the rest are members of our congregation. I don't think we'll have any problem."

"You *think?*" the captain asked. "How strongly is that?"

"I can assure you," Burton said.

I looked at his face. He meant it.

"Besides, you never gave us official permission," I said. "And if there is any litigation, Burton and I will assume full responsibility."

"Then we shall do it," he said. He turned on the loudspeaker that connected to every room on the ship. "This is Captain Robert speaking. All passengers are please asked to assemble in the theater in ten minutes." He repeated the announcement twice.

His voice carried well. In my cabin I heard it every day five minutes before each meal. No one could miss it anywhere on the ship.

To my amazement, everyone was present before the expiration of the ten minutes. I wondered if they had all been sitting in their cabins waiting for something to happen. Probably not, but I sensed a tension among them.

Burton counted to make sure no one was missing. "There were forty-seven passengers because Twila did not have a roommate. We have lost two people, so that should be forty-five." He finished and said, "All accounted for."

As soon as Burton assured him that we had forty-five passengers in the room, Captain Robert stood up. "Ladies and gentlemen, thank you for coming." He made about a thirty-second speech to apologize for our having to return to South America, saying, "In view of the sad circumstances, I am most certain each of you understands." He concluded by saying, "As you know, Dr. Burton and Dr. West have investigated this deplorable situation as a personal favor to me. They now have something to report to you."

He turned toward us and waved at me to come forward. I had previously asked to sit near the door. "It may not be necessary, but as a precaution," I had said.

I explained to the entire group about Twila's book of lectures. On a whim, I asked, "Is there anyone here who doesn't know about the lectures and the book she was writing?"

"Everybody knows," Jeff said. "The gossip mill has spread it everywhere."

"You didn't specifically ask us not to say anything," Sue said, "but common sense would say we should hold everything in confidence."

"I, for one, did not say a word." Jeff stared at Betty.

"I didn't realize it wasn't —"

"It doesn't matter," Burton said. "In fact, it saves us explanation." He smiled at Betty.

"So someone killed Twila because he or she didn't want to be in the book?" Mickey asked. "That's strange, because all that person had to do was say, 'Take me out,' and she would have done it."

"That's not exactly the reason," I said.

"What is the reason?" Jon asked.

"I'll answer that later," I said.

"I'll bet all of us, or at least most of us," Pat said, "were Twila's patients —"

"Clients! We're clients. It's a kinder word," Betty yelled.

"Okay, clients. Whatever!" Pat said. "And for everyone's information I would never kill Twila or anyone."

"I'm in her book, but I would never, never, never kill her!" Jeff yelled.

I heard a couple of other voices say the same thing. I waited. *Oh God,* I silently prayed, *please, please help me right now.*

"Are you going to accuse me of killing Twila just because I'm in her book?" shouted Jon.

"We're making no accusation just yet," Burton said.

"But we expect to be able to have some concrete evidence to show who killed Twila and Heather," I added. "Before we reach Ushuaia tomorrow."

"And this is also to tell you," I said, "that none of you needs to be afraid. I assure you: There is no danger of any further deaths."

Burton stared at me, and our gazes locked. I saw the beginning of a smile escape his lips. He nodded slightly.

"There's one more person we need to talk to, isn't there?" Burton whispered. "I think I finally got it."

I'm not sure what the Cheshire-cat smile is, but I think that's what I gave him.

38

I turned to Captain Robert and said, "I think we can dismiss everyone." He looked at me strangely, and I said sotto voce, "Stay here. We have one person with whom we need to speak."

"What? You call us down here just to tell us *nothing?*" Donny said. "What is going on?"

"I resent this kind of strange behavior," Shirley said. "If you have some vital clue or urgent information —"

"Why did you call all of us here?" Jon asked.

"All right," Burton said. "Please forgive any inconvenience. I'll explain later why we did things this way."

We both heard grumbling, but Burton tried to assure everyone. "Trust us," he said several times.

Captain Robert talked to several people, and so did Burton and I. However, I watched the one person I wanted to stay. I realized Burton was doing the same thing. Burton had figured it out. As soon as that person reached the door, I leaned over and said, "Can you wait until the others leave?"

"Oh, I can wait for you anytime," he said and gave me a full grin.

It took perhaps three minutes before everyone left the room. Once they were all gone, I walked over to where Jon Friesen was seated. "Jon, I asked you to stay because I have a question for you."

"Anything. Or I could ask you a few questions — a few very personal questions."

"Ah, but I'm first," I said and smiled.

"Go right ahead."

"I'm curious about something. How did you know Twila was writing about you?"

"Word got around that she was going to write about all her patients — her clients."

"You mean you heard that on board the ship?"

"Nah! I knew before we left. The word had circulated, so we knew."

"Everyone knew? All of you?"

"Probably not all, but the word got around that she was going to use us in her lectures, and afterward she'd polish it and have it published."

"How did you know?"

He shrugged. "All of us knew. It wasn't any big secret." He shook his head. "Can you believe it? Some of them were delighted to have her spread their names all over the world."

"Some people like publicity of any kind," Burton said. I knew he was making conversation and waiting for me to take the lead.

"But how did you know?" I asked. "Did Twila tell you? About the book?"

"I don't remember the details, except —"

"Did she tell you that you were one of the people in her lectures?"

"Maybe not directly, I mean, I *know* I'm one of those she chose. Why wouldn't she want me in her lectures and her book?"

"Good question," Burton said. "I assume you have rare qualities and presented a unique case for her."

"Unique. Yes, that's true." He seemed to preen as he answered.

"Did she ask you to sign a permission slip?" I asked.

He blinked, and the easygoing manner seemed to slide away from him. "I don't remember signing one, but I may have. I signed a number of papers. Twila was always shoving a paper in front of me to sign."

"Who told you — the first one who told you — what Twila was doing?" I asked.

"Hmm. Will I get someone in trouble if I tell you?"

"*You* may get into trouble if you don't tell me." I thought that was a brilliant response. "We think we know who killed Twila and Heather, but we need your help."

"Of course I'll help you." The smile was in place again.

"And — ?" Burton asked.

"Betty Freeman. Please. I don't want to get her into trouble. You see, she had a long talk with Twila and asked her to make some changes."

"Because Twila painted her too — too dark?"

Jon roared. "Too dark. No, she didn't think it was dark enough. She felt she had been in far worse shape before she started treatment. So, yeah, that's how I found out."

"Anything you can tell us about Betty and the lectures — the book?"

"She told me she had second thoughts and wasn't sure she wanted to be in Twila's book."

"When was that? When did she tell you?" Burton asked.

Jon stared into space for a few seconds. "That first landing. King George Island. Yeah, that's when it was. On the Zodiac going over."

"Was she upset? I mean, really upset?"

Jon eyed me cautiously. "I'm not going to get Betty into any serious trouble, am I?"

"I don't think so," I answered.

"In that case, she was really ticked. She didn't explain why, but she kept saying she needed to talk to Twila and straighten something out." He looked into my eyes and said, "You don't think Betty would — ?"

"People react strangely when they're angry or upset," Burton said.

"Yeah, yeah, they do."

Just to keep him off balance, the way good lawyers and detectives work, I asked, "Did Twila ever say specifically that you were in the book?"

"No, I mean, not in so many words, but I knew."

"How did you know?"

"I just knew."

"But Twila didn't say so." I kept my voice calm and I hoped conversational, so he wouldn't know how important his answers were.

"Not in so many words." He looked at me, and just then it seemed as if the lights came on inside his brain. "You knew I didn't sign a permission form, didn't you?"

"It was a good guess."

"Did you ask Twila if you were in the

book?" Burton stepped closer. He handled the question well and in such a casual way he might have asked about the weather.

"Yes, as a matter of fact, I did. That made me angry — not angry enough to — to hurt her or anything like —"

"But angry."

"It's my life, isn't it? If she was going to teach and write about me, didn't I have the right to know?"

"Of course you did," Burton said in a smooth, quiet voice. "It's a normal question. Why wasn't she open with you?"

"I don't know. Honest. I don't know. But I asked."

"What did she say?" Burton was a trifle too eager, but I didn't think Jon picked up on it.

"She said, 'That is none of your business.' Can you imagine that? None of my business. It was *my life*."

Neither of us said anything to Jon. The captain, as an objective observer, sat silently and listened to everything. For several minutes Jon ranted. He called Twila unprofessional, unfeeling, uncaring. He said she only wanted to make money from her clients and report their cases so she could become a big star in her field. His voice grew louder. He slammed my chair twice with his fist.

I interrupted with the pseudo Carl Rogers approach that first-year students at the university used. "You're really quite angry now, aren't you?"

"Wouldn't you be upset? Of course I was upset. I had planned to talk to her about it, but — well, you know, someone else must have been even more ticked off than I was."

Burton said nothing, but his facial expression was such that Jon felt secure enough to continue ranting.

Jon used a lot of profanity before he stopped abruptly. "I'm sorry, Pastor. You're a man of God and all, and —"

"I've heard those words before," Burton said.

Good for you, darling, I thought. *That was a perfect answer.*

I wasn't aware how long Jon yelled, but his anger increased instead of diminishing. That's typical of a person in his condition. After a while, even the profanity became repetitive, so I said, "You are so angry, Jon. Her actions really upset you."

He stopped in midsentence and slumped in a chair.

Now I knew.

His extreme anger made it clear that he hadn't benefited from his therapy.

39

"Excuse me just a second, will you?" I said to Jon.

"If I must — but don't go too far."

"Oh, I'm not going far," I said. Despite my anger, I gave him a fairly decent smile. "I need to speak with the captain about something."

I walked across the room and tried to sound as if I were whispering to him. "He's the one. We think Jon Friesen killed Twila and Heather."

"I heard that! You are crazy! You're the one who needs a psychiatrist. You're crazy, you know!"

Burton moved right in front of Jon and put his arm on the man's shoulder. "I certainly hear your protests. She's made a strong assertion about you."

Jon swore and called me the worst names that seemed to rush into his head. "I thought you loved me," he said. "I thought

— well, I thought we had something going for us!"

I thought he was going to spit at me.

"I'm glad I found out now about who you really are."

"I think we can settle this," Burton said. "It's very easy, you know. And if Julie is wrong, I shall insist that she apologize to you."

"Thank you, Burton. You are a friend. A true friend."

I thought Jon was going to hug him. Instead, he extended his hand and shook Burton's.

I wanted to smile. Burton had gotten my message even though I had not said one word to him. "So how does Jon prove that you've falsely accused him?"

"Simple," I said. "We can search his room."

"Would I kill a couple of people and keep the weapon?" Jon leered at me.

"Let's search his room anyway," I said.

"Search my body first," Jon said. "I might have some weapon on me."

I nodded to Captain Robert to do just that. I was sure Jon didn't have the evidence on his person, or he wouldn't have been so insistent that we search him.

But I wasn't looking for the murder

weapon. I was sure he had disposed of that.

The captain patted him down. I wondered if that was something they taught sea captains or if he had seen the same movies I had.

"Let's go to your room." I said the words in a commanding tone. "If I'm wrong, I'll get down on my knees and apologize."

Jon snickered like a ten-year-old boy. "I'd really like to see that!"

"Then let's go," I said.

Burton led the way, and Jon swaggered behind him. I say *swaggered,* but both had to hold on to the railing because the ship was really heaving and rocking wildly.

"Do you think he has the knife — or whatever it was — in his room?" the captain asked me softly.

"No, I don't," I said. "I think we need to assume that he threw it overboard."

"Or I didn't have any weapon," Jon said. "I heard that. So if I threw a knife overboard, why would you search my room?"

"There is something else — something that I think we will find inside your room."

"Oh, and what would that be?"

"A camera," Burton said. "Unless you've thrown that away." He winked at me.

I frowned at Burton, but I thought, *You really don't miss much.*

"You think you're so brilliant!" Jon shouted. "You won't find a camera in my room. I didn't kill anybody."

"Wow, that sounds just like the dialogue on a TV series called *The Closer* that had reruns just before we left."

Jon dropped his head. It was obvious he had watched the same episode, and I'd caught him.

"The man on that show was innocent," I said. "Remember?"

"And so am I."

"Prove me wrong!" I didn't wait for an answer but moved ahead of him and Burton. "Which cabin?"

"Twelve," he said.

I walked in first, and Jon came in right behind me. "I gotta see this. I gotta see you find something that *isn't* in my cabin."

Burton and the captain flanked each other and followed. The sea was still rough, so I held on to the guardrail. Jon saw me turn my head and look at him, so he tried to tough it out, but about the fifth step, he lurched forward and grabbed the railing just before he fell. Burton hugged the rail without trying to prove anything. The captain must have had what the sailors call sea legs. I looked back and saw that his body made the slightest weight adjustment with each step he took. It wasn't a conscious shift, but I assume it had come after years of sailing across the Weddell Sea.

The captain opened the door to cabin twelve. Jeff Adams lay on his back in his bunk. He had a book in his hand, but I think he had been asleep. "Please let us have the room for a few minutes," the captain said.

Jeff's gaze shifted from one of us to the other before he got out of bed. He grabbed his book and left without saying anything.

"Let the captain search," I told Burton. "If he finds the evidence, Jon can never say we planted it."

"There is nothing to find! Nothing to find! Nothing to find!" Jon yelled. "All this accusation and there's nothing to find!"

"Sit on Jeff's bunk." Burton's strong voice implied that it was not a matter for discussion.

Jon sat quietly with an expression somewhere between a smirk and a grin as the captain searched. I had the utmost certainty that the evidence was in Jon's cabin. The camera was small, but I was sure we would find it.

Without his being aware, from the corner of my eye, I followed Jon's gaze. His eyes flared briefly when the captain picked up the shaving kit, opened it, saw nothing, and put it down.

Jon relaxed. "Keep looking. Do you plan to spend the night?"

"Captain, empty everything from the shaving kit onto the bunk," I said.

Without asking the reason, the captain did so. He began to sort through everything. Then I saw *it.*

Now it was my turn to smirk.

40

Jon didn't have a camera. I assumed he had thrown Heather's away. That had been a smart move. In a small plastic bag was a black object about the size of a postage stamp.

"That's the evidence," I said and pointed to the object.

"What is it?" asked the captain.

Jon closed his eyes.

"It is the camera's memory card," Burton said.

"It's so small," I said, "Jon wouldn't have had any trouble getting ashore with that."

"Thank you, Captain," Burton said. "We had expected to find Heather's camera, but I'm sure we can find someone on the ship with a digital camera that this memory card will fit."

"They're fairly universal," I said. "So you shouldn't have a problem."

"I'll make an announcement and ask

286

anyone with a digital camera to bring it to the theater." The captain turned to Jon. "Sit. You can't run away, so just sit on this bunk until I return."

Jon sat in a hunched position, his eyes closed.

The captain left the room.

Less than two minutes later, the captain made the announcement over the intercom. Perhaps another ten minutes passed before he came back to the cabin with four digital cameras. The memory card fit in the third one.

We turned on the camera and stared at what we saw. Heather had taken perhaps a dozen pictures at Brown Bluff. We were particularly interested in six of them. The first showed two figures, dressed in blue, walking toward the hillock. One of them was taller and wore his life jacket. The next picture was about the same, but in the third one, Jon had grabbed Twila's arm and we could see his profile and hers.

The fourth picture showed them walking over the rise. In the fifth picture, Jon had turned his face and we clearly saw him. He was coming back alone. He wasn't wearing a life jacket. In the sixth frame, we had a clearer view of his face. The time frame at the bottom told us that the entire ordeal had taken slightly under seven minutes.

"Do you wish to tell us what happened?" The captain asked.

Jon hugged his body and pulled his legs in tightly on the bunk. He rolled over and lay in the fetal position.

"I'll explain it, then," I said and turned to Captain Robert. "You have the right to correct me, Jon, if I'm wrong."

He remained in the fetal position with his eyes closed.

"I have to guess about a few things — I mean, up until the killing. That much we can prove."

"No question about that," Captain Robert said. "I shall be most happy to write a deposition for you."

I thanked him and said, "Here's what happened." I smiled because I was sure I must have sounded exactly like Jessica Fletcher as she explained how she put the clues together to catch the culprit.

"It began with a simple assumption: Jon wrongly assumed that Twila had included him in the book." I paused and said, "I'm not sure why — maybe he was angry because he didn't like the way he *assumed* she portrayed him."

"You have no idea, do you?" Jon said, but he didn't move.

"No, but I'm sure it was something trivial." I gazed at Burton. The shocked look on his face made me feel good. "Something more normal people wouldn't have thought twice about."

"Trivial? If only you knew," Jon said.

"Maybe we're not bright enough to figure it out," Burton said, "but nothing is important enough to kill for."

I wanted to see if I could make a Jessica Fletcher script actually happen, so I said, "After all, you are a mental patient."

"I was. I'm cured."

"Oh, that's what the nutcases say?"

Burton's mouth opened, but he caught on and said nothing.

"You think you know just about everything, don't you?" Jon sat up in bed. "You have no idea why I killed her."

"The book — your mistaken assumption —"

"That's not what I meant," he said.

"What did you mean?"

"She knew. I thought she would tell."

"Knew what?" I feigned indifference. "It couldn't have been much —"

"I loved you, did you know that?" Jon yelled. "I loved you. I was willing to marry you!"

Now I knew he really was a borderline

personality. I sat down on the bunk beside him. "And I'm not worthy of your love. Right?"

"Just like the others," he said, and he focused on me with that unblinking stare.

I heard something — something ominous — in the way he said, "Just like the others." Any good therapist automatically listens to the tone of the voice, perhaps even more than the words. "What about the others?" I said in my quiet, professional voice. "Twila found out, didn't she?"

He nodded.

"How did she find out?"

"I did something stupid — I mean, really, really stupid."

"You told her? Is that it?"

"How did you know?"

I didn't know, but I was trusting my intuitive sense on this one. "She was your doctor, and you felt you could trust her . . . that she'd never tell . . . and you were safe."

"That's exactly right! She led me on! She made me feel I could say anything, and I would be safe."

"But weren't you safe? Did she betray you in some way?"

"Worse."

I must have frowned, because I was momentarily lost.

"So you don't know everything, do you?"

"She may not be as bright as you are," Burton said. He spoke with exactly the right tone that invited trust.

"I told her — about the others — about my first three wives —"

"That you killed them?" Those words just slipped out of my mouth, but as I said them, I knew they were right.

"Yes, I killed them. Do you want to know how I did it? No one suspected me. I was far, far more clever than the police."

I didn't want to know, but Burton said, still in that calm voice, "Yes, tell us how you outwitted everyone."

Jon got up and paced the small cabin. *Paced* may not be the correct word, but his movement reminded me of the way a lion walks around in a cage. He spoke faster and faster, and at times Burton calmly asked him to say something again.

"Fascinating, isn't it?" Jon said.

"Oh, that it is," I said perhaps a little too skeptically, but he didn't catch the sarcasm in my voice.

He had married three times and in three different parts of the country. The marriages started fine, but (in his words) in each case his wife became difficult and constantly nagged him. They fought. He beat up the first one, and she called the police. He knew he had to be careful. So he made up with her. "She believed me." They lived in Colorado and decided to sell everything and move to Florida.

He killed her along the way, weighted down her body, and dropped her off a bridge along the Mississippi River. He moved, instead of Florida, to Kentucky. The second wife he dumped in the Ohio River. For the third wife, he rented a motorboat at St. Petersburg and pushed her off into the Gulf of Mexico.

He went into vivid detail about what he had done, explaining that no one had ever tracked him down. He wrote to friends in various places and told them that his wife had met someone else and left him.

"But I made one big, big, stupid, stupid mistake: I trusted Twila."

"Did she threaten to turn you in?" I asked.

"No, she couldn't do that." He winked. "Doctor-client privilege."

"Oh," I said.

"But she bugged me again and again. 'You need to make this right,' she would say to me. Almost every time she saw me, she said something like that. But I fixed her —"

I was ready to say, "So you killed her?" but I hesitated.

"No, see, I planned to take care of her. I smuggled a knife in the bottom of my luggage. I was going to kill her and toss her overboard, but she never walked on the deck alone. When I tried to talk to her, she insisted on sitting in the lounge."

He said that after he saw how they did landings on the *Vaschenko,* it was easy to lure her. On the Zodiac, he whispered to her that he was ready to turn himself in when they got back, but he needed to talk to her about something first.

He got her away from the others. As they walked along, she began to resist him and said she didn't believe him. He grabbed her and told her he wouldn't hurt her. "She believed me then," he said with a satisfied smile.

After that it was simple. He stabbed Twila six times to be sure she was gone. He dropped his life jacket next to her body so there wouldn't be an extra one on the beach and made his way back to the others.

He saw Heather, but at the time he didn't realize she had taken his picture. "Or there might have been two bodies left on Brown Bluff."

"So you waited until Ivan was distracted on the VHF radio to the ship, got behind him, and said that two passengers were sick and were going back on the third Zodiac." I stopped and turned to Jon. "How am I doing so far?"

"You make it sound easy. It worked because I was clever. I had vomited on board the ship before we went. Three people saw me. That was clever, wasn't it?"

"Oh yes," I said. "I would say that showed how cleverly you planned everything."

"Ivan was the only weak part of the plan. But it worked easier than I thought."

"Obviously," I said.

"You got into the other boat and probably induced your own vomiting again so there would be no question about your being sick," Burton said.

"I want to be clear about one thing." The captain spoke for the first time. "You killed the woman — Ms. Wilson — because of the pictures? Is that not so?"

"You might as well admit it," I said. "We have enough circumstantial evidence."

"We have everything but an actual picture of the murders taking place," Burton said.

"But that's good enough," the captain said.

"So the reason for killing Heather —"

"Don't go stupid on me now," Jon said.

We stood silently around the bunk. I wasn't sure what to do next. We had him —

I knew that, and so did Burton and the captain.

"You are saying, then, are you not, that you also took the life of Ms. Wilson?" Captain Robert said.

He shrugged. "What is it they say about if you're going to hang for a chicken, you might as well hang for a cow?"

I had never heard that before and wasn't sure it made sense. But it didn't have to make sense to me.

"All right, I did it," Jon said in a faint voice. He sounded like a child. "Twila wanted to ruin my life. She was going to put everything about me in her book."

"You're wrong," I said.

"You're not in the book," Burton added.

"How do you know that?" His eyes popped open wide, and he stared at me. "What do you mean? Not in the book? How can that be?"

"Because we have identified all twenty-one people. You're not one of them."

"That is a lie!"

"I'll show you." I poked my hand into my shoulder bag and pulled out the list and held it out to him.

He snatched the paper from me. His whole head moved as he read down the list.

"My assumption is that Twila thought you

were either too far beyond her help, or —"

I watched the movement of Jon's eyes as he read down the page, reached the bottom, and went through the list again. He screamed and wadded up the paper with his left hand and struck out at me with his right.

Burton grabbed his left hand and twisted his wrist. "Let go of the paper."

It didn't take much pressure before he dropped the single sheet. I folded it. "We know all the information," I said, "so you couldn't have destroyed anything significant."

41

I might as well tell you the rest of Jon Friesen's story. I hesitated because this honestly sounds like the conclusion of *Diagnosis: Murder* or *Murder, She Wrote* where they corner a criminal and he cries out something like "You have to believe me because I didn't mean . . . ," or some silly babble. It's a clear, neat ending for a TV script that has a forty-eight-minute time length for each episode.

Life isn't usually that clean; however, in this case Jon finally said he wanted to talk to me. Alone.

I told Burton it was all right, and the other two went outside the cabin and closed the door.

"You know I love you, don't you?" he asked. "I saw the way you looked at me at church."

This was true paranoia speaking, and I sat down on the bunk across from him. He confessed his love to me several times. When

I mentioned his affair with Heather, he said, "She meant nothing to me. It was you — only you that I wanted."

I believed that he believed his own words right then. In an hour he probably wouldn't.

He began to ramble about not trusting people, especially shrinks. "She didn't turn me in and said she wouldn't, but she begged me to give myself up. I told her I wasn't ever going to do it again — you know, hurt anyone." He rambled then about forgiveness because he had asked God to forgive him, and if what Burton preached was true, he was forgiven.

I wanted to say that I was sure Burton also pointed out that we have to take responsibility for our wrongdoing and pay the penalty.

I didn't.

He seemed to calm down and said, "You know what she told me?"

I shook my head.

"She said I have no conscience!" His voice began to rise again. "Who did she think she was to say that?"

"Is it true?" I hadn't meant to say that, but the words popped out.

He stared blankly at first before he said, "I guess that's true. I don't regret killing any of them."

"So you killed your former wives —"

"They were an inconvenience —"

"I'm sure of that."

"If only Heather hadn't been so under-handed and scheming. And demanding. That was the worst part: her demands."

"Demands?" I echoed.

"Yes, she wanted to marry me or —"

"Oh." I had no idea what else to say.

Jon went into another tirade about Heather, and I let him talk. This time it must have gone on for twenty minutes. I didn't understand it all, but I think he mixed up Heather with his mother and a sister and someone else. Or maybe I just couldn't follow his nonlinear ranting.

He finally shut up and sat quietly on his bunk for a few seconds. Then, as if he had flipped the switch, he said, "So that's over. What's next?" His voice was as casual as if he asked, "What's next on the menu?"

"I know you don't get it, but this is an extremely sad and painful time for me," I said. "Twila had only a short time to live, and you killed her."

I told him about her cancer.

He giggled. He actually giggled. "Then I saved her a lot of pain, didn't I?"

Burton opened the door just then. The captain and two crewmen were behind him.

I wouldn't have killed Jon, but I would have hit him. As it was, I burst into tears and couldn't stop sobbing for a long time. Burton's warm, comforting arms finally calmed me. He led me to my cabin. He had Betty bring the doctor, who offered me a tranquilizer. I refused it and lay on my bunk and sobbed as if I could cry out all the pain.

I cried for peace, but none came.

After what seemed like hours, exhaustion set in and I felt myself drift slowly to sleep.

42

When the ship docked at Ushuaia, the Argentinean police stood at the foot of the gangplank, ready to arrest Jon. An American official, who I assumed was the ambassador, was with them. Even though the murder took place in international waters, Thomas said Argentina claimed ownership of that part of the world. "They must decide whether to try him in South America or in North America." He spat over the side of the ship and added, "For two killings, does it make any difference where the trial happens?"

I didn't want to hear any more of his speculation, so I walked away.

We stood on the deck but couldn't leave the ship until they took Jon away. No one told us anything.

As soon as he was off the ship, Jon stopped and waved to all of us. Despite his handcuffs, his arms waved wildly. To their credit, no one waved back. No one spoke. He said something to the police and looked back at us. He yelled something at us. I was glad we couldn't hear what he said.

On the return flight from Ushuaia to Buenos Aires, Burton sat next to me in Twila's vacant seat. Neither of us said a word until we were airborne.

"How are you feeling?" He turned to me with those soft, pastoral-looking eyes, and I had to look away.

"How do you think I feel?" I realized I had an edge to my voice. "I've lost the dearest friend in my life."

To his credit, he didn't say, "I know just how you feel," or some inane remark. Instead, he took both my hands before I could pull them away. He prayed for me and asked God to grant me peace and to soften my sense of loss.

I cried again, but this time the pain wasn't as deep. I missed Twila — and I knew I would miss her for a long time — but his prayer brought solace. I don't know how it's possible to be at peace and to cry at the same time, but that's what I did.

"Thank you." As soon as I was aware that he still held my hands, I pulled them away. A flicker of pain crossed his face.

"Julie, I —"

"Don't," I said. "I love you. You have done so much for me. I'm a serious Christian today — maybe not a good one, but I'm learning."

"There is definitely a *but* at the end of that sentence," he said softly.

"And you know what it is." I turned my face away from him. "Please leave my life. I don't want to see you again until —"

"You did say *until?*"

"Yes, of course."

"I'll call you," he said.

He didn't change seats but remained next to me for the rest of the flight. Our plane was late pulling into the gate, but I didn't say a word to him for the three hours we were together.

On the flight to Atlanta, he changed seats again and sat beside me. I watched movies and he listened to music. We sat as if we were total strangers. Once his leg brushed mine and he apologized.

The plane landed in Atlanta, and we still hadn't spoken. I wished he had stayed in his own assigned seat. I couldn't help but look at him. He needed a haircut, and after all those hours on the plane, his dark facial hair made it look as if he had started to grow a beard.

He was on the aisle and stood up. He looked at me and said, "May I get your bag from the overhead compartment?"

I shook my head. "Please, I don't want to see you or hear from you until."

He nodded and went forward with the crowd. I waited until the aisle was empty before I got up and retrieved my bag. A couple of minutes later, I spotted him in a line at customs, but he was quite a distance ahead of me. By the time I had my luggage and got to the taxi stand, he was gone. I shared a cab with Betty Freeman.

Betty gurgled over the wonderful trip, and I smiled whenever she paused. I didn't hear anything she said. My mind flitted between my grief for Twila and my love for Burton.

Dear God, if You don't mind listening to me, please help Burton. He really needs You.

My cell rang on Friday morning, which was the third day after our return from Antarctica.

"It is Until Day," he said.

"You're sure?"

"You said I couldn't call until. Remember?"

I started to cry softly. I couldn't help it. Two or three times he tried to explain, but my sobbing increased.

"I can't talk —" Fresh tears stopped me from saying anything else. I hung up.

Afterward I wondered if Burton understood my tears.

43

Saturday morning the doorbell rang just before seven o'clock. I knew who it was just by the three short rings.

I had barely gotten in from my morning run and was perspiring, but I opened the door.

"I know, I know," he said. "You just got in." Before I could answer, he said, "I parked across the street and waited for you to come back." He held a bag from Starbucks. "Vanilla latte and a chocolate bagel for you," he said. "Black with a spoon of milk and a raisin bagel for me."

I had spotted his car across the street but pretended I hadn't.

"You'll have to sit at the breakfast table while I shower."

He sat down, and I hurried to my bedroom. I closed the door, and fresh tears came. But this time, I prayed. I prayed out loud. It was the first time in my life that I had ever done that.

"Thank you, God." I said the words several times.

And something else happened: I knew God heard me. I didn't know where this would end, but I knew God had heard me pray. And I knew I had a true talking-praying relationship with the Lord.

"So that's what people mean when they talk about touching heaven," I said to myself.

For once, I had no smart remark to make to myself.

"I think it's time I talked to my parents," Burton said. He set down his cup of unfinished coffee and stared at me. Those blue eyes showed such sorrow that my maternal instincts wanted to grab him and soothe him. This wasn't the time to soothe him.

"With me? Without me?" I asked.

"I can't do it unless you're there. You know everything anyway."

"You're sure? Really sure that you're ready?"

He didn't answer. The grim set of his jaw was the only response I needed.

"As soon as you can get dressed, we'll drive there."

"I am dressed," I said. I wore my only pair

of Donna Karan jeans that flattered my amorphous figure better than anything I'd ever owned. They were topped by a simple pale green sweater with Kelly green piping. I had hesitated about earrings and finally wore tiny gold ones. And sandals, of course. With Burton always flat shoes.

He smiled and embraced me. "You know, the few times I was able to hold you in Antarctica, I missed the fragrance of your perfume."

"Why waste it?" I said. "Besides, I didn't know I'd let you hold me."

He smiled. "I knew."

"Oh, and how did you know?"

"Twila told me. She assured me — no, she actually promised me as if she had been able to look into some kind of magic fortune cookie —"

"That's because she loved us both," I said. "I don't think she saw it. I think she wanted it to happen."

He kissed my cheek. "So did God."

The Burtons live in Woodstock, which was close to an hour's drive for us from Clayton County on the south side of Atlanta.

Burton had finished his coffee and swallowed the last of his bagel. "Whenever," he said.

"I'm ready. I'll finish my latte in the car."

By the time we left Riverdale and headed up the east side of I-285, I had drunk the rest of my coffee and decided I was too nervous to finish the bagel. I put it in the bag for garbage.

Burton handed me his cell. He refuses to talk while he's driving, and I like that about him. I opened the cell and thumbed down until I found their number. "Hi, this is Julie West — you know, Burton's friend —"

That was all I needed to say. His mother, Marianne, was a warm, talkative soul. "So when are you coming to see us?" she asked.

"Strange you should ask. I'm in Burton's car right now. We're on the way. I estimate about thirty-five minutes."

"Thank you for coming with him," she said and asked me questions about the cruise. I promised we'd tell her details after we arrived.

That satisfied Marianne. Before she hung up, she said, "I'll have coffee and fresh muffins ready for you."

That was Burton's mom. I had liked her the first time we met. She was slender, maybe five three. I'm sure most people looked at the family and assumed that he had gotten the smile and those blue eyes from her. The elder James Burton had dark, curly hair. He was about an inch taller than I was. On the few occasions I had been with him, I always said, "You're a man to whom I can look up."

He liked that.

James Burton was quiet — and he'd have to be with a lively wife like Marianne. But one thing I liked about him: When he did speak, he always had something to say.

Nearly forty minutes later, we arrived at his parents' house. I knew Burton had kept the speed down, and I told him, "You drive as if you want to prolong the time until the moment of truth."

"Moment of truth? From which TV show did you pick that one up?"

"I don't remember, but it has a nice ring to it."

If his face hadn't been so grimly set, I think he would have smiled.

His father was James Burton Jr., and Burton hadn't wanted to be called the Third or Trip, so he asked everyone to call him Burton. James and Marianne had called their son Burton from the time he was about three years old.

Burton hadn't said more than three or four sentences on the drive. I knew he was lost in his own tortured soul.

We pulled up to the main entrance of a gated community with a guardhouse and two security guards staffing it. Even though both of us had been there before and Burton recognized one of the guards, we still had to show them our IDs. One guard scrutinized our drivers' licenses while the other guard phoned the Burtons' house.

He handed us back our licenses. "You take a left at the top —"

"I know where it is," Burton said.

"— of the hill. That's Twelve Oaks. Go two streets and take the next left on Tara Trace. It's the second house, number 107." He held out a clipboard for Burton to sign. After the signature, he saluted us. "Sorry, Burton, but I got reprimanded a month ago for being friendly."

"It's okay," I said. "We understand."

The house on Tara Trace was not only large but also two stories high, and I think it must have had six bedrooms. (I never asked.) It looked like something out of *Gone with the Wind*. But then, that was the idea. It had four immense white columns in front, and the building was made of weathered red brick. As we pulled up, I saw the open garage and a Mercedes parked next to a sleek-looking sports car.

We walked up the eight steps to the im-

311

mense front porch that went halfway around the house. The front door was made of thick dark cherrywood and flanked on each side by narrow leaded windows.

We had barely gotten to the door before it flew open, and Marianne Burton rushed forward and hugged both of us. She wore a simple pale pink pantsuit that probably cost more than everything I wore. She wore one thin, scalloped gold necklace with matching earrings. I liked the simplicity of her clothes. I had no doubt that everything she wore was expensive, but her clothes were what I call subtly elegant.

James Burton Jr. stood at the door and waited his turn so he could embrace us both.

"You're the finest woman he's ever brought here," he whispered and chuckled. "Come to think of it, you're the only one." He wore a blue blazer, white trousers, and a silk shirt with an ascot tied at the neck. On most men it would have look pretentious; on James Burton Jr., it looked natural.

James brought us immediately into the living room, which was a cluster of huge English Chippendale wing chairs and Irish Chippendale side tables in front of the fireplace. I don't know much about furniture, but I know my Chippendales.

After we sat down, Marianne brought coffee and hot bran muffins on a tray. She and her husband had tea, but they served us coffee.

"So you went to Antarctica?" Marianne said. "I'm sure it was lovely — I mean, what you saw of it."

I knew she and James had been there a decade earlier, so I added, "I don't imagine anything has changed."

"Not there."

Burton sat quietly. He gave one- or two-word answers if asked, but otherwise he sipped his coffee slowly. He left his muffin untouched.

For perhaps twenty minutes, Marianne and I talked about everything that had happened in Antarctica. They had gone from Australia and seen the larger, emperor penguins but admitted they hadn't seen nearly as much wildlife as we had.

After a few minutes, the conversation lagged. To her credit, Marianne stayed cheerful. She asked about Twila, expressed sympathy, and then asked about Jon Friesen. CNN had said he was being sent back to Atlanta for trial. "We also read about it in the papers. Terrible, terrible."

"Yes, it was," Burton said.

That time he spoke three words. But it

was obvious he wasn't going to say more.

Marianne cleared away the coffee and muffin crumbs and came back to the table. "Okay, son, what is it? Something's bothering you very, very much." She smiled and said, "I don't have to be a mother to detect the sad face."

Burton looked at her and then at his father. The love those eyes showed toward him touched me. I wished I had grown up in a family with that kind of warmth.

"I have something to tell you," he said. "Something that's not easy for me to talk about — but I have to say it."

Ordinarily I would have immediately made some smart remark to relieve the tension, but this time Burton didn't need any distraction.

"Let's sit in the den," James said. "It's more intimate." We followed him into the room. The furniture was every bit as expensive — or at least it looked expensive to me, but it had a warmth about it. Two walls were lined with bookcases, a third wall was mostly window, and the fourth wall housed another fireplace. It wasn't cold enough for a fire, but it felt cheery sitting in a semicircle.

For at least a full minute, no one said anything. I heard the ticking of the grandfather clock from the room we had just left.

"Do you remember Dan Rosenberry?" Burton asked.

"How could we ever forget him?" Marianne said. She turned to me. "Burton and Dan were inseparable friends. I mean, like twins —"

I knew that, but I smiled and asked, "That close?"

"Oh yes, they did everything together. Burton never had a sibling, so we welcomed Dan."

"I think he slept here more than he slept at home," James said.

Marianne leaned forward. "Just to fill you in, Julie, Dan had a terrible childhood. His dad was an alcoholic, and I think his mother drank a little —"

"She drank about as much as he did," Burton said in a soft but unemotional voice.

"The boys were about the same size," Marianne said. "They shared each other's clothes constantly —"

"Primarily, Dan shared Burton's," his father said. "Most of Dan's clothes weren't very good." He smiled and said, "I don't mean that to sound snobbish. His clothes were faded, small holes in his sweaters, sometimes his shirts lacked buttons, that sort of thing."

"That's right," she said. "I had forgotten. We loved the boy. We truly did. In fact, by the time they were in fourth grade when we bought new clothes for Burton, we frequently bought clothes for Dan. But his mother just couldn't seem to keep them in good condition. Despite all of that, he was a sweet kid."

"His parents," James said, "were rather strange. Both parents worked — that is, both worked some of the time —"

"They had a special ability to get fired," Burton said. I was surprised at the lack of emotion in his voice. "She couldn't get to work sober, and he argued with everyone."

"But Dan was special. Yes, he was very, very special," Marianne said. "He was also bright — in fact, he was probably a little smarter than our Burton."

"That's true," Burton said, "but most of all, I loved him, you know. He was —" His voice broke, and he pulled out a handkerchief and wiped his eyes.

"That's what made the loss so bad for you." Marianne patted his hand. "The accident was such a terrible, terrible blow for you. I wasn't sure you'd ever recover. And all those months you spent in the hospital —"

"That's what I want to talk about," Bur-

ton said. "I need to tell you about the accident."

44

"Are you sure you want to?" the elder Burton asked. "We'll listen, of course, but we know how much you loved him, and it hurts us to see you in pain."

"You don't have to tell us anything," Marianne said. The tone of her voice sounded odd, and I couldn't figure out what she meant. "Sometimes it's best to leave the past behind and to move on."

"Yes, son," James said, "it's all right not to go into the accident."

"I have to tell you. I have to explain — explain things no one else knows — I mean, except Julie. There's something — something I did. Something wrong — really wrong — and I've carried it all these years. I need to tell *you,* most of all."

James walked over, pulled Burton to his feet, and hugged him. That didn't seem characteristic of him, so it was obvious James sensed that this was a terrible confession Burton had to make. "I hope you know we love you, son. No matter what you have to tell us."

Burton held James's shoulders, and I thought Burton's heart had broken. I suppose it had. Many people have come to my office over the years and cried, and some of them reminded me of wounded animals, wailing in despair. I had never heard such convulsive crying from a man before.

As I watched, and despite my resolve, tears cascaded down my face. I was so proud of Burton. At last he was going to tell the truth. I thought of a verse in the Bible — although I had no idea where it was — that said the truth would set people free.

Marianne clasped my hand. Her grip was so tight I finally had to pull it away to get the circulation going again.

I don't know how long Burton cried on his dad's shoulder. It was probably only four or five minutes. I didn't think about time; I thought about Burton's pain, something he had carried for almost twenty years.

Burton sat on the sofa next to me and took my hand. "I have to tell you this. It's hard on me, and I know it will be harder on you, but I owe you the truth."

"You're sure?" Marianne said.

"I have to tell you."

45

Both boys were ten years old, although Burton was younger by four months. A few days before Christmas, Dan Rosenberry's father decided he wanted to put up a live Christmas tree. His father told him that they had not been able to afford one since Dan was a baby. Things were different now. He had a good job and had been with the same company ten months, which was the longest Dan ever remembered his dad keeping a job.

His mother had worked steadily at a convenience store for a couple of months and had been sober when she went to work.

Instead of buying a tree, Randolph, Dan's father, decided it would look nicer (and save money) to drive north of Atlanta to the mountains near Dawsonville. Dan's father had heard that there were many good trees of the right size less than a mile off the road.

"They're just waiting for someone to claim them."

"But that's stealing —"

"Shut your mouth," Wanda Maxine Rosenberry said.

"I don't plan to pay for no tree while they're just standing alongside the road, begging for someone to take them."

Dan knew better than to argue.

They took both Dan and his best friend for the big tree-hunting event. They also carried a large supply of beer and popped open one bottle after another.

Randolph drove his ten-year-old Honda Accord about twenty miles over the speed limit. Once in a while he'd get so caught up in his beer, the speed would drop down, but then he would abruptly speed up again.

Both boys knew it wasn't wise to say anything. Dan had once commented on the speed, and Randolph slapped his son and sped up more. Dan never said anything again about it. Burton whispered that he felt better not looking at the speedometer.

Shortly after they left the south side of Atlanta, the first raindrops landed softly on the windshield and ran downward in hesitant streams. The farther north they drove, the more intense the rain became. Before long, hard spikes of rain made tuneless music against the top of the Honda. From the distant mountains came the ominous, rhythmic booming of a storm. It was getting worse.

"Heavy rain ain't no big deal," Randolph said. "Only sissies are afraid of a little wet stuff."

The air had grown colder, and the rain turned into sleet. They were going steadily uphill and around tight curves, but Randolph didn't slow down. Soon the barren trees were jacketed in glittering ice. Bare, black branches poked from beneath the outer layers like shattered bones.

"Honey, you might be going a little fast for the curves," his wife said.

"Just shut up. Hand me another beer and leave the driving to me!"

The two boys sat in the backseat. Dan hugged himself and bunched into a corner.

"You cold?" Burton asked.

"A little." His jacket was hardly warm enough for the temperature that hovered just above freezing. Randolph refused to use heat in the car. "Suck it in, boys!" he yelled back at them. "Cold weather makes you strong."

"If I had a hundred extra pounds on my body, I'd feel the same way," Burton whispered to his friend.

Dan's teeth began to chatter.

Burton took off his heavy, hooded jacket. "Here, put this on. It's plenty warm."

"But you'll get cold."

"When I do, I'll ask for it back," Burton said.

Dan smiled gratefully and they exchanged jackets.

A little later, Randolph stopped on private property that was far enough from the main road or from any house so that no one would see them. He walked around and seemed not to notice the stinging sleet. The boys wanted to stay in the car, but he wouldn't let them. "See how a real man works," Randolph said. He grabbed his gas-powered chain saw and paced an area of about fifty feet until he found exactly the tree he wanted. He circled the tree several times. Wanda Rosenberry pulled her cotton coat tighter. "Yeah, fine. Just get it."

"This is some beauty," he said and started the saw going. The sleet had not let up and a few snow flurries mingled with the sleet. The boys wanted to go back to the car. "Just stand there and see how a man works!" he repeated.

It took less than a minute for the tree to fall, and its icy blanket shattered on the ground.

He made the boys grab the top and help him carry the tree back to the car. "Don't want to drag it on the ground," he said. Burton had gloves and Dan didn't. "Keep your hands in your pocket," Burton whispered. "I'll do it." By then, he was also wearing the hooded jacket again.

Randolph tied the tree across the top of the car with the ropes through the two front windows. The trip going back was even colder with half an inch of space for the sleet to come into the vehicle.

Dan's teeth began to chatter. The boys decided they would alternate wearing Burton's jacket every ten minutes. Burton handed him his watch (Dan had none). "Put it on and you watch the time. When the ten minutes are up, you give me back the jacket and the watch."

Dan smiled gratefully and said, "This makes a good game."

Before they got back on the main road, both of Dan's parents drank four more bottles of beer, and his mother opened a new case. They started driving south.

The flurries grew heavier. The windshield wipers could barely keep up with the white flakes. The more beer Dan's parents put away, the more erratic the driving became. Several times Randolph swerved across the road into the other lane.

Burton opened his mouth to say something, but Dan put his hand on his sleeve and whispered, "Don't. It will make it worse."

"So what do we do?"

"Pray, I guess," Dan said. He scrunched down in the seat behind his father, hoping that being out of the path of the wind and wearing the hooded jacket would help him warm up before he had to return it.

Events after that weren't clear. The police report said that Randolph Rosenberry, age forty-nine, driving south on Georgia Highway 400, attempted to pass a slow-moving Ford pickup on an upward curve. He crossed the double yellow lines to make the pass. He barely passed the truck and reached the top of the incline when a school bus appeared heading north. Rosenberry pressed his foot on the brake. Either the car skidded on the icy road, or he turned the wheel too far to the right to get back into his lane. No one was sure about that part.

The car ran off the road and down an embankment. The police records stated the drop was ninety-eight feet. When the vehicle hit bottom, the speedometer stopped at eighty-six miles per hour. The Honda landed on its side with the passenger side smashed on the ground and glass spattered all through the car.

Both of Dan's parents had been smoking. The report said that as far as they could tell, one or both of the cigarettes ignited their clothes or their upholstery. Within minutes after the car hit the bottom of the ravine, the entire interior of the car was aflame.

The driver of the bus stopped his vehicle and started to rush down the embankment. It was dangerous getting to the car. He fell twice. When he finally reached the burning car, the door behind the driver was partially open, so he reached inside and grabbed the first body he saw and carried it about twenty feet away. By then, two other men had also stopped and raced down to the scene.

Someone pulled out a second body — the driver. He was breathing and his arms flailed.

Because of the spread of the flames, the three men weren't able to get to the other two people still inside the car. Someone rushed down to them with a fire extinguisher. It didn't matter; their bodies were so badly burned that no one would have been able to recognize them.

The first survivor, a boy, was unconscious. His face was smashed from the impact, and heavy shards of glass were wedged into his face and skull. Third-degree burns covered both legs and later required grafting. On his arms were first- and second-degree burns. His right arm was broken, and he had contusions and minor lacerations all over his body.

The boy awakened in the hospital. His face was wrapped in bandages and his arm in a sling. Every part of his body cried out in pain.

"Good afternoon," the nurse said. "Are you ready to stay awake now?"

He nodded. "I — I don't know what —"

"Shh, be quiet," she said. "Your parents are in the waiting room. I'll call them. They've been here almost around the clock."

"Am I going to die?"

"No, you're going to be fine."

"My friend —"

"Shh, you rest now." She checked his IV, flicked it with her finger. "Relax. You're going to be fine, but you need to rest."

He wanted to cry out and ask what happened, but he fell asleep.

When he awakened, the doctor was examining him. The nurse pulled the thermometer from his mouth. "Normal," she said and smiled. "First time."

"Well, you've had quite a journey, haven't you?" the doctor asked.

"What happened?"

The doctor turned, and the boy saw the Burtons holding each other. "You tell him," James Burton said.

"The car ran off the road," the doctor said. "Your friend Dan died instantly; so did his mother. His father survived about two hours, and we couldn't save him."

"Just me?"

"Yes, only you," the doctor said. "And we weren't sure about you at first. Your injuries were quite substantial —"

The doctor patted the edge of the bed. "But you'll be fine now. You'll have to stay with us for a while, but I think we can fix you up."

"Just me?" the boy asked again.

"Just you." The doctor's voice cracked as he added, "Your parents identified you because of your jacket and your watch with your name engraved on the backside. Your face was so badly damaged, no one would have been able to recognize you. By using pictures from your parents, we've tried to reconstruct your face. We can't make you quite as pretty as —"

"When? When did it happen?" the boy asked.

"Six days ago," the nurse said. "You've been unconscious most of the time."

"Six days?" The boy heard the words, but the meaning eluded him. "I don't understand."

"Your parents tell us they call you Burton. Just rest, son. You're alive."

"But what about — ?"

"Your friend died, and so did his parents."

"Dead? Dead?" the boy asked again.

He remembered nothing after that. He must have drifted off again. When he awakened, his room was dark. Only lights of the city shone into his room.

As the boy lay there, the meaning of the words sunk in. He was the only survivor. The doctor said that all three Rosenberrys were dead.

All three?

They think I'm Burton.

He lay quietly as that thought filled his mind. "They think I'm Burton," he said aloud.

46

Sleep eluded Dan for the rest of the night. "This isn't right," he kept saying to himself. "I'm Dan. I'm the only survivor. I can't let them think I'm Burton."

He was too worn out to do anything. In the morning he would tell them the truth. He had lost his parents; they had lost their son.

But as he drifted into sleep, he thought of what it would be like to be James Burton the Third.

He knew his parents hadn't been good parents. He had seen too many examples of happy families, normal people like the Burtons. So many times he had yearned to have a family like that. He used to daydream that he had been adopted or stolen, and his real parents found him. They would love him, and he'd never have to worry about having decent clothes or enough food to eat.

He was almost asleep before he asked

himself, "Why can't I? Why can't I become Burton? By the time they fix my face, no one will ever know." They were about the same size, same color hair and eyes. People had sometimes called them brothers or even twins.

"No one will ever know."

He said those words aloud several times.

"Besides, I don't have anyplace to go." Tears seeped out of his eyes. He felt he had never really had anyplace to go except the Burtons'. They lived in a big house only four streets away from the run-down apartment his parents rented. "They wouldn't want me if they thought I was Dan."

The two had been close friends since they met in first grade. Burton had no brothers or sisters. Dan was an only child. There had been a sister, but she died when he was three or four. If he had other relatives, he didn't know about them.

"And the Burtons have nobody," he said.

Again and again he thought about the situation. *I don't have anyone in the world who knows me. My parents are dead. And my old man was nothing but a drunk anyway. Mom was a little nicer, but she was just as bad a drunk.*

"What do I have to go home to?" he asked aloud. "I don't even have a place to go. Who would want me?"

He became suddenly alert and thought about the situation. If they believed he was Burton, he could have parents — real parents — people who would love him. He wouldn't have to lie to the apartment manager about why they couldn't pay the rent. He wouldn't have to beg the owner of the liquor store to let his parents have just one more six-pack.

"I'm Burton," he said aloud. "I'm James Burton the Third."

For the next three hours he tried to think of everything Burton had told him and what he had observed in the home. "I'll be Burton."

His face was in such bad shape that it took four surgeries before Dan resembled the pictures of James Burton the Third. Nearly six weeks passed before he went "home."

For a long time he tried not to think about what he had done. He became extremely quiet for several weeks. He tried to absorb as much information as he could about the family and especially about Burton. He didn't want to make a mistake.

His "parents" took him to their church. After he became a believer, he went through a communicants' class. The pastor assured him that if he confessed his sins, God had forgiven him.

"All my sins?" the boy asked. "Even the worst, worst sins in the whole world?"

"Yes, Burton, even the worst of the worst."

It was the first time he had felt at peace since the surgery.

After that, the new Burton blossomed. His grades at school were near the top. Burton hadn't been as good a student as Dan, so he emphasized how hard he studied so he could bring home better grades.

The Burtons never questioned his identity. They showered the same warmth and love on him that he had seen them display toward Burton.

He became a better listener, and for several years, he remained afraid that he would be exposed. But the pastor's words slowly eased themselves into his heart. "I am forgiven," he said. "Jesus Christ has forgiven every sin."

Those words brought deep peace.

For a long time the pastor's assurance had been enough. It wasn't until he was in seminary that he began to think of the consequences. He had lied. He had deceived the Burtons.

He hadn't told anyone except Roger Harden, who was dead. And then Julie, whom he loved.

Roger Harden had seen Burton's grades. He had the eleventh highest grade-point average in his graduating class. Eleventh. He could have been number one, but he was afraid that would expose him.

Too late he realized that if he had made only a slightly better GPA, he would have received a full scholarship to Yale, something Roger Harden offered to only one student each year.

Harden sought him out, and they talked for a long time. He was a man in his midfifties, and he had a way of listening to people that immediately enabled them to trust him. Burton liked Roger, and the older man offered him a scholarship to any school he wanted to attend. He chose Wheaton College, which is in a western suburb of Chicago.

Over the next two years, Dan-now-Burton felt a kinship with Roger. At Christmas after his first year, the student came home to Woodstock, where the Burtons now lived. But the first opportunity he had, he visited Roger at his office in midtown Atlanta.

Roger spent nearly three hours with the young man.

"What's wrong with you, son?" the man

asked. "You look so sad."

"I did something bad — really bad."

It was the first time Dan felt he could trust someone with the truth. With tears streaming down his face, he told Roger Harden the truth.

"That's not so bad. You want my suggestion?"

"Of course. It's been a big burden all these years."

"Say nothing. You can't hurt anybody but your new parents, right?"

"But it's not right. I lied. I stole their son's identity."

"So you want to tell them now? After all these years? As far as they are concerned, you're their son. Don't hurt them."

Roger Harden needed almost an hour to persuade Burton not to tell.

With his head in his hands, Burton finished the story. "I love Julie, and I want to marry her. I need to make this right with God and with you. She said she wouldn't marry me until I do. She pushed me to do the right thing."

"I don't want to marry him with this on his conscience," I said. "I love him, and — and I know it hurts you —"

Burton paused and pulled out a handkerchief. "I'm sorry. So sorry. I love you, and I didn't mean to hurt you or to deceive you —"

James pulled Burton to his feet. "We love you. We've always loved you. That can't change." He kissed Burton's cheek. "Of course we forgive you."

"But I've deceived you for nearly twenty years. I know this must hurt you — but I can't — can't live with the lie any longer."

"We forgive you, son. We love you. It makes no difference to us," James said. "You have been our son. You are our son."

Burton nodded slowly, and tears fell again. When he was able to talk again, he knelt in front of Marianne. "Please forgive —"

"I love you. You have been a wonderful son to us," she said.

"How can you be so — so kind and forgiving when I've been so deceitful?"

Marianne looked at her husband, and he nodded.

She hugged Dan tightly. "We knew, *son*. We always knew."

With a dazed look on his face, Burton stared at her. He tried several times to speak, but the words seemed stuck in his throat. His lips trembled, and tears filled his dark blue eyes.

"Parents just have a sixth sense about their own child," James said.

"You had been so close to Burton, and we loved you, too," Marianne said. "You know that, don't you?"

Burton nodded twice, and more tears flowed down his cheeks.

"You had no one to take care of you." Her voice cracked before she added, "And we had lost our only child."

James cleared his throat before he said, "It seemed to us that's what Burton would have wanted us to do."

EPILOGUE

Everybody likes a happy ending.

And this story also has a happy ending.

First, we consulted the Burtons' family lawyer about the Dan Rosenberry–James Burton III thing. Although he agreed with us that there would probably never be any legal or ethical repercussions, Dan-cum-James should officially change his name. He did.

He also recommended that Marianne and James officially adopt James "to forestall any further legal problems."

They did.

By then, we had been back from Antarctica for six months, and my grief over Twila had begun to heal. I still miss Twila — and I think there is a hole in my heart that will never heal.

Burton asked me to marry him, and I said yes with three tonal variations and in five languages.

Burton thanked me in all five languages.

I wanted the formal Episcopal wedding ceremony, and Burton was all right with that — he's amazingly agreeable about most things. He said no only to one thing. I wanted to have three bridesmaids — which wasn't a problem, but I wanted to have two of them and leave the middle space open in memory of Twila.

"Twila is not here. You may miss her," Burton said, "but she is not here. Theologically, I wouldn't be comfortable with that."

That's Burton. When he says he wouldn't be comfortable, that's his soft way of saying no. So we compromised when I said, "We'll name our first girl Twila."

"I would be comfortable with that."

On March 23, we had our wedding. Burton contacted his best friend from his seminary days, Dr. James Martin, and he agreed to perform the ceremony.

I loved the language of the vows so much I memorized them.

Dr. Martin told Burton to face me and take my right hand before he repeated these words: "I, James Burton III, take thee, Julie West, to be my wedded wife, to have and to hold from this day forward, for better or for worse, for richer or for poorer, in sickness and in health, to love and to cherish, till

340

death do us part, according to God's ordinance; and thereto I pledge thee my troth."

Burton released my hand. We still faced each other, and I took his right hand in mine and repeated these words: "I, Julie West, take thee, James Burton III, to be my wedded husband, to have and to hold from this day forward, for better or for worse, for richer or for poorer, in sickness and in health, to love and to cherish, till death do us part, according to God's ordinance; and thereto I pledge thee my troth."

During the rest of the ceremony, right up until the kiss, our eyes focused on each other. Never in my life had I felt so loved. I felt as if I were the most blessed person in the world: I had Burton's love, and I knew God loved me.

Surely nothing would mar our happiness — not even another murder.

ABOUT THE AUTHOR

When **Cecil Murphey** isn't plotting murder, he writes or cowrites books such as *90 Minutes in Heaven* (written for Don Piper), which has sold more than three million copies. He has written such nonfiction books as *When Someone You Love Has Cancer* and two books on Antarctica, including *With Byrd at the Bottom of the World* (the story of Richard Byrd's historic Antarctic expedition of 1928–1930, cowritten with Norman D. Vaughan). Please visit his Web site at www.cecilmurphey.com.

You may correspond with this author by writing:

Cecil Murphey
Author Relations
PO Box 721
Uhrichsville, OH 44683